I0699636

The Heart of Family

Rebecca Matley

Contents

Dedicated to Nat and Viv who taught me so much about the world
and how great God is.
Though I hold your little hands, you both hold my heart.

CHAPTER ONE

Philippa squeezed her eyes shut as she counted down from five. Opening her eyes, the world of bright light and color-coordinated tables filled her senses. The smell of crayons and stale glue were somehow stronger with her eyes open. All her eight-year-old students were still too engrossed in their crafts and conversations to notice that she had discreetly moved Mr. Waffles behind her large desk. Mr. Waffles was the large golden retriever stuffed animal that was the class mascot. He always came out when the class was doing well but with today being the last day of school, Philippa knew without a doubt that if the third graders saw him on their way out, they would all break down and want to hold him. The students would never get to their parents on time, and she would be stuck having to explain to Mr. Rogers, the principal, why Mr. Waffles should be allowed to return next year. And he needed to return next year. There was no better motivator for a child than a stuffed animal.

Philippa turned back to her class and put on her teacher's smile. While she was still considered new, her teacher's smile was now completely natural to her. The more uplifting twist in her voice that she thought often of as her teacher's voice also came naturally. These days, it was more of a struggle to not use her teacher's voice in conversation. And yet, while she had become used to her new teacher quirks, she had yet to become used to the shenanigans her third graders always got into.

So, when Harry, Charlie, and Pete were giggling and constantly looking under their desks, Philippa's nerves rose, and her teacher's smile seemed to freeze onto her face. *Let's see. The pencil cup is still in the corner, the reading corner homophones are in their box, and the math center still has all fifteen of the white boards. I packed the math magnets this morning, the sandbox was off limits today due to an incident at recess, and Mr. Waffles is still safely behind my desk.* Her nerves clinked together in her mind as she took the eight steps to reach the boys' desks. *What did they do?*

"Boys." Philippa put on her "serious teacher" face, clasping her hands together to create a more formal representation of herself. "What are you three hiding under your desks?" Harry and Pete snickered, but Charlie had the decency to look almost ashamed as the boys pulled a huge ball of shoes out.

"We tied our shoes together!" Pete declared.

Philippa sighed and tried to maintain her composure. "Why would you do that?" She wanted to ask, "*Why would you do that an hour before school gets out for the summer?!*" but decided against it, as a reminder of summer was only going to hype up her almost calm class.

The boys shrugged and handed Phillipa the shoes. "We already tried untying them, but they're stuck together," Charlie nodded at the entwined laces. "Sorry, Ms. Carol."

Philippa studied the knot of black, red, and green laces and held in a groan. They really had done a number on their laces, but thankfully the laces were thick enough that it wasn't as bad as it could be. Honestly, the knots she and her sister used to have to wiggle their necklaces out of were ten times worse, but to have such a needlessly complex problem on an already chaotic day was just the icing on top of a fast-melting ice cream cake.

"Alright, here is what we'll do. I will unknot these while you three get back to working on your project. If I see one more shenanigan then I am going to put each of you at separate desks, understood?"

The threat of separation was enough to cow all three of them, and they meekly muttered "Yes, Ms. Carol." and turned back to their craft.

Philippa nodded in approval and turned to the project at hand, the three pairs of shoes dangling from her hand. She sighed as she pulled the red pencil from her dark, inky black hair, her bun falling out in shoulder length locks around her. She began by wedging the pencil into the nooks and crannies of the knots, trying to loosen the monstrosity as best she could. Only five minutes passed when she finally felt victory.

With the shoes unknotted, Philippa handed each pair back to their owner. It wasn't hard to guess whose shoe was whose. Charlie's shoes were the smallest as he had yet to have the growth spurt the other two had had. Harry's had Spiderguy on them, the superhero the young boy idolized. That left Pete's shoes; black with a neon green stripe around the edges. The boys mumbled a thank you and hurriedly put their shoes back on, intent on getting back to their project and conversations. Philippa made her rounds, strolling through the room, going between desks. She was careful to complement each student and their work, absentmindedly noting how the class conversations had shifted from plans for the summer, to the pets they had and the ones they wished they had.

Philippa chuckled to herself as she turned back to her desk. One of her students, Synethia, wished she had a pet snake. Philippa didn't know Synethia's family very well, but the thought of her high-class and proper mother even being near a snake was hard to imagine.

Philippa sat at her desk and simply watched her students work. Their chaos had overwhelmed her at the beginning of the year, but now it was hard to imagine two months without having the easily distracted kids. Her classroom, which she had slowly been prepping for summer, looked almost empty without her grammar and math posters up, or the fairy lights that used to line the white board. Her bulletin boards, which used to be covered in bright colors and displays of her students' work, were now empty and bare. Philippa's heart twisted at the sight. She liked the idea of a fresh start, but she hated endings.

She shook away her sadness, pushing up her large black glasses. *Why is this so hard? I knew this was coming! There's a large portion of time that I spent dreaming of this day. But now that it's here... I'm going to miss them.* She smiled softly at her kids, not the teacher's smile but a real true smile. *I need to thank God for the time I had with them. I can't just live in sorrow. I need to take advantage of this moment and praise Him for the time that I had with these wonderful kids.*

"Ms. Carol! Tommy stuck his tongue out at me!"

"No, I didn't!"

"Yes, you did!"

"No, I was just pretending I was my dog!"

"Why pretend to be a dog when you already are one?"

Philippa pushed down her smile, hiding her joy in having something to distract her. Yes, the year was ending, and soon all of her comedically chaotic kids would be gone, but so would their little fights. She took a deep breath and put on her teacher's stance. It was time to get back to work.

Philippa leaned out of her classroom door, sighing in relief when the last two parents came down the hall.

"Charlie, Pete, your parents are here to pick you up."

The boys, sitting in the bones of what used to be the math center groaned but gathered their things. The boys had gotten close over the last few months, as they were always the last to be picked up. Pete's mother was usually late because her job was across town, and she always managed to get stuck at a red light or four. Charlie's dad was always late for everything he did. Philippa didn't know much about the family, but she knew Charlie's dad was a little too obsessed with work. Charlie's mother, who picked him up once or twice a month, had ranted to her about that fault many times while Charlie gathered his papers.

Pete shocked Philippa by giving her a bone crushing hug. "I don't want to go to a new classroom Ms. Carol. I want to come back here on Monday."

Philippa leaned down and wrapped her arms around the small boy that had nearly been the end of her. "I know. This year was fun, but I bet fourth grade is going to be even more fun."

"No, it won't," he stubbornly sniffled.

"There's only one way to find out. How about, after the first day of fourth grade, with your mother's permission, you visit me and tell me all about your summer and fourth grade. I'm sure Mr. Waffles would love to see you again."

"Okay," he sighed.

"Come on, Pete," his mother called to him. "Remember, your dad just bought a new game. The faster we get home, the sooner you get to play it," she baited.

By the light in his eyes, Philippa could tell it had worked. He gave her one last hug then ran the three steps to his mother. Charlie was the next to hug her, taking Pete's spot almost immediately. "I'll come visit you too, Ms. Carol."

Philippa smiled and squeezed the little boy. "I'm looking forward to it."

"Charlie, come. I must drop you off at home and then get back to work," Mr. Johnson, Charlie's father, grumbled. Mr. Johnson stared at Charlie, wearing the ever-present narrowed expression that matched his stiff suit.

Charlie nodded, his little lip trembling as he left her arms and crossed the short distance to stand next to his father. Philippa watched as Pete held his mother's hand while talking about all that he had done that day, a small skip to his step. Meanwhile, Charlie kept a two-foot distance from his father while they walked in silence, waving goodbye to his friend.

She waited until the families were out of sight before she closed her door and leaned against it, creating a mental list of all she had left to pack up before leaving. *I need to put away the center tools, wipe down the desks, and vacuum. Then I should be all good until August.* With her mental list made, she began to tackle the center clean up. The desk centers were just little baskets filled with colored pencils, glue, and little safety scissors, all of which were sticky

In the middle of putting away the colored pencils, the door opened and in came Mrs. White. Philippa knew that as a fellow teacher she could call the old woman Gwen, but for some reason, Mrs. White fit her more. The old woman had fluffy white hair that curled around her ears and brilliant blue eyes that always struck everyone who saw them. She had the habit of wearing pencil skirts and knit sweaters, even in this awful summer heat. The old woman was sweet as could be but always was trying to fix everyone's life. Her newest project: Philippa Carol.

"Hello, dear. Still finishing cleanup?" Her voice rang, her words sounding like a song as she pulled her hair behind her ear, the small curl bouncing back out of hiding

Philippa stood up to greet the old woman. "Yes, I had to wait for two of my students to be picked up."

"Ah, I understand. The same two as always?"

"Yes, but both parents made it here at the same time, so neither one was bored here."

"That's good."

"Have you finished packing?"

"Yes, I had the kids play a cleanup game."

"Oh, I should have done that. I'll make sure to take a note of it for next year."

"Ah, so you are staying for the next school year?"

"Yes. I told you that the teaching abroad thing wouldn't happen until the year after."

"Have you heard whether or not you've been accepted?"

Philippa tried unsuccessfully to hide her smile. "I may have gotten the acceptance letter yesterday." Philippa had dreamed of teaching English in China since she was a junior in high school. The dream was a bright light she could always see guiding her, and she felt drawn closer to it. The warmth it radiated, the ability to share the hope that lived within her with kids across the world; it was a constant companion. A mission's trip that would give her the opportunity to teach English and to share the hope she found in

Jesus. She had been saving for years, but with college debt being a thing, her China trip had been put on the back burner. It was only with the strong encouragement of her sister that she had decided to apply now, rather than wait and save money for a few years.

"Goodness, Philippa, this is fantastic news! Why have you waited this long to tell me? At your age, I would have screamed it at everyone I knew."

"Well, because I may have been accepted, but that doesn't mean I can go. I need to make a bunch of money this summer in order to accept it in September. It wouldn't be right to accept it and then not be able to afford it, wasting a spot someone else could fill." Philippa looked down at the pen that was in her hands, twisting the cap on and off. Money was not the only reason she hesitated. Since moving to this town, Philippa had found a community of people that she loved and that loved her. If she left, would she be able to have such close relationships again? *Life has been really good here. Why change a thing?* But still she felt pulled to this ministry.

"Yes, but the hard part is over!"

Philippa shook away the somber, more emotional excuses. "Unfortunately, not. I don't have any clue how to make enough money in only two and a half months. There aren't many places that are hiring for just the summer. And even if I work at the coffee shop, there is no way I could ever make enough money."

"You have a good point. Have you looked into tutoring?"

"Yes, but it wouldn't move me even an inch closer to my goal." Philippa sighed and put her box of colored pencils and box of glue sticks into the little red wagon that she had wheeled in during lunch. "I'm afraid I'm going to have to reject it and try again next year."

Mrs. White pursed her lips, taking a disinfecting wipe and beginning the vigorous project of cleaning the desks. "Let me see what I can do."

Philippa laughed and shook her head. "You are very kind, but my problems are my own. Don't trouble yourself. I have already decided to trust God in it." *Change is scary, it always has been. But God's plan is greater than mine. I will strive to get the money but if I don't then I will trust that God wants me here. And if He provides the money, then I will follow where He is calling me.*

"You are quite right. But I shall still see how I can help anyhow."

Philippa's heart warmed at the old woman's kindness. "Thank you."

"Yes, well, you won't be getting anywhere if we don't stop dilly-dallying and start cleaning."

The two laughed, going back to work. Philippa looked at the quickly emptying room and smiled. This classroom was full of wonder and knowledge all in one, and the desire to bring such wonder for education to China burned brighter within her.

Chapter Two

Though she had given the situation to God, Philippa's heart was still heavy as she went to church that Sunday. But looking up at the familiar building eased some of the knots in her stomach. Sitting between a parking lot and knolls of grass, the crème cement church sat in its simplicity. There were no imposing gargoyles or spirals to a bell tower like she had seen in other churches. No, this building was a simple block building with an open gable chestnut roof. The only thing that interrupted its simplicity was the river rock siding that lined the lower four feet of the building's walls. Stepping onto the rock path that led to the building, Philippa counted ten of the blessings she had had just that morning.

...Seven, I made it here without getting into a car crash. Eight, the school year ended so smoothly. Nine, I am able to worship God openly without worry of being arrested. She took the last step to the door. *Ten, I get to teach kids at Church today.* Philippa put her hand upon the chestnut door and took a breath before pulling

it open. The open door revealed the large lobby. The lobby was crème with cool wooden floors. The main desk stood in the center of the room, an oak table with pens and paper, the event chart, and the bulletin upon it. To the left were two other tables that had been flooded with pastries and a variety of coffee options. Philippa grinned, aiming herself for the front desk, stopping in front of it and the woman who was behind it. Charice, Philippa's best friend, jumped out of her chair and threw her arms over the desk and around Philippa.

Charice was vibrant in every sense of the word. She was always in loud colors with a matching headband to hold back the massive puff ball that was her hair, and she was usually two degrees louder than the rest of the room. Philippa secretly thought this was why Pastor Tom had asked Charice to work the welcome desk. Everyone knew how loud the lobby could get on Sunday mornings. Even now, an entire half hour before the service was scheduled to start, the lobby was full of different voices. The worship team must have just finished practice because Dave, the worship leader, was the loudest and only voice she could truly discern from the others.

"Philippa! Girl, where have you been? I haven't seen you since Wednesday!" Wednesday nights were Philippa's second favorite day of the week. Every Wednesday night her church held prayer meetings, always in one family of the congregation's houses. Philippa loved the feeling of being welcome into people's homes. It was good to see her church friends in a more intimate setting, and it was lovely to be able to pray with them.

"That was only four days ago. Less than that!" Philippa pulled out of the hug and fixed her glasses.

"Days! That is much too long. We should do something more often!" Charice's gold hoops hit her neck as she overdramatically shook her head. The gold metal reflected the light so her warm coco skin almost glowed. "But let's take advantage of this moment and give a cheer for your acceptance into teaching abroad."

"Let me guess, Mrs. White told you."

"Yes."

Philippa chuckled. "The second I told her, I knew she would spread the word."

"That's Mrs. White for you."

"Well, I don't suppose she told you that I will probably have to reject the offer."

"Why would you have to do that? Are you doubting yourself? Because you don't need to. Just three days ago you made the very wise, mature decision to pick up a coffee for me! And I am super picky! If you can do that, then you can definitely go across the world."

"Is that supposed to be a hint that you want coffee?"

"You are so good at reading my mind!"

Philippa giggled, moving to the next table to get a Styrofoam cup of coffee for her odd friend. She handed the cup to Charice who had pulled out a bottle of hazelnut syrup from her purse. Philippa watched in amusement as Charice pulled a small metal container out of her bag and poured froth from its depths over her coffee.

"Sorry, I should have grabbed your coffee first. Now I know why you were excited to see me." Philippa folded her hands in front of her, struggling to resist the urge to pull her hair up with the pen she kept in the pocket of her floral dress.

Charice took a sip of her coffee and hummed her enjoyment. "Ah, coffee. The sweet nectar God has given to hold us over until Heaven."

Philippa almost snorted out a laugh but instead gave a small nod. "Anyway, back to our earlier conversation, I'm not doubting myself."

"What other reason could there be?"

"Money."

"Ah," Charice clucked, leaning back into her stool. "Yes, that would be the venom that has taken over. I completely understand why money is the root of all evil."

"You're only saying that because they raised the price of coffee at Linda's two weeks ago."

"I have had to live without constant caffeine for two weeks! Why would they charge so much for the basic necessity of living?"

"Probably because it's not a basic necessity of living. Unfortunately, if I don't make most of the money by September, then I will have to refuse."

Charice slowly sipped at her drink, her eyes squinting in thought. Philippa waited patiently, knowing that Charice wasn't going to respond until she had something useful to say. "So, that means you need a high paying summer job."

Philippa nodded, her hair—that she had painstakingly curled in the morning, already deflating into her naturally pin straight hair— falling forward, drowning her heart shaped face.

"Have you thought about becoming a nanny for the Johnsons?"

"The Johnsons?" Charlie, Philippa's student over the past year, came to mind. She rarely saw him and his family at church. They were usually late and always left early. Though, from the few glances she caught of them, they always were dressed well and smiling. A decent and wholesome family. Philippa knew little else about them.

"Yeah, haven't you heard?" Charice didn't even wait for Philippa's head to shake no. She knew how little Philippa liked to gossip. "The Johnson's are getting divorced. They are living together for now, but the divorce and custody trial will be finalized in September."

"What? But how? They always seemed so happy." *Divorce.* Memories of her parents' divorce flooded her system. Sadness, the heavy kind that followed those memories, weighed down upon Philippa's heart. As a child of divorce, she had an idea of the mountain of pain they were going through. *Poor little Charlie.* She could perfectly picture the small boy hiding all alone. *And doesn't he have an older sister?* The idea of the two kids living through the breaking of a home was enough to turn Philippa's stomach sour.

Charice continued, unaware of the pain that coursed through Philippa. "No one's certain as to why they're getting divorced. But it looks like it's a mutual split. Their last nanny quit abruptly, so it sounds like they're trying to get a replacement a.s.a.p."

"Are they not able to be with the kids during this time?"

"Mr. Johnson is working in pharmaceuticals while the Mrs. is an emergency room nurse, and you know how crazy busy and short staffed the medical field is."

Philippa thought back to her family during the divorce but immediately pushed them to the back of her mind. It was true that the medical field had been requiring a lot of hours lately. *But is that the reason they're working so many hours?*

In a flash, against her efforts and will, came the memory of her parents choosing to divorce. Every day the divorce was getting finalized was filled with hours of loneliness. They were working. Somehow, they were never able to be home for more than a few hours. They were *gone.* Philippa shook her head, brushing away the memories. *Even if it doesn't pay as well as Charice seems to think, I have to help them.* Philippa fiddled her fingers together, pursing her lips at the thought of poor Charlie and his sister being all alone. *God, please be with this family. Grant them peace and strength during this time. Amen.*

"I want to help them, though, there is the problem of contacting them. I'm in charge of kids church today and they always keep their kids in the sermon."

"I can help with that."

Philippa jumped at the sudden new voice, turning to see who had been listening in.

"Ah, Mrs. White. How are you this morning?" Charice asked, sipping her almost empty cup of coffee. She didn't look at all surprised to see Mrs. White, but Philippa's heart was still beating out of her chest at the woman's sudden appearance.

"Doing just fine, dear. My old bones have been creaking all morning, it's a miracle I heard you two talking over their creaking."

Philippa simply smiled, but Charice laughed. "Mrs. White, you could hear private conversations if you lost both of your ears."

Mrs. White chuckled. "It is a terrible habit. It's something I have struggled with all of my life. But this time it may have come in handy. I happen to be a good friend of Angela Johnson. We text all the time. I will put in a good word and see if I can get you a job interview."

Philippa bit her lower lip. The desire to help Charlie and his sister was strong but something in her hesitated. Her confidence in helping them withered under this odd feeling. *Could I really go back into the kind of situation I've been running from for so long?* "I don't know. This feels very sudden. Let me think about it for the rest of the day, and I'll let you know by tomorrow. Is that alright?"

"That sounds like a wise plan. It would be no good to get into a situation and then not be able to leave." Mrs. White daintily sipped her tea, the white Styrofoam cup crinkling in her hand.

Charice looked down and frowned. "My coffee is all gone. What a tragedy! I need more caffeine before the sermon."

"Too late," Philippa chuckled, nodding over to the small TV hooked up to the corner of the lobby. The TV showcased a countdown to the service, and it currently was at the one-minute mark.

"Oh, no!" She turned and put her hand to her forehead. "You see, Philippa? This is what happens when we hang out. I lose track of time and waste precious moments that I could be using to focus on coffee!"

Mrs. White leaned over and lightly patted Charice's hand. "You will be fine, dear."

Charice groaned, gathering her Bible and purse. "If only that were true!"

The moment Charice was out from behind her desk, Philippa hooked her arm through the crook in her friend's. "Come on. We can stand next to each other during worship. If you want, you can even help me teach children's church."

"I definitely didn't drink enough coffee to do that!"

Philippa laughed; her heart lighter than it had been a minute ago. The joy of worship was always increased when she was around loved ones. The worry and stress over the Johnson family could wait until after church. For the next hour and a half, she only had one focus—growing in her faith and helping those around her to do so as well.

Chapter Three

Philippa paced in her apartment's living room. She still hadn't been able to figure out what the odd feeling was that made her hesitate. She knew she wanted to help them, but still she paused.

Come on. Why must everything be so complicated? It's not like the Johnsons are anything to be worried about. They have a good respectable reputation. But then, why am I so afraid? Philippa stopped her pacing, struck by the realization of what the feeling was. She was afraid. *Why am I scared? There is nothing to fear.* Her self-reasoning did nothing to help her. The feeling, the *fear*, coiled around her like a snake. She sighed, her breath blowing the whisps of hair that had fallen from her bun out of her face. She let her gaze slide to the large window that centered her living room's green tea walls. The sun was setting, bleeding its orange light onto her sheer curtains with little flowers she had embroidered into them. Philippa looked out at the world that was slowly changing from sunlight to city light.

What do I do? She stopped her pacing and instead came to sit in front of her window, crossing her legs under her as she sat on the carpeted floor.

Lord, her prayer began, but stopped at the lack of knowing how to continue. It took a moment or two before she could continue. *I don't know what to do. I want to help them. I want to be with the kids during this hard time. But I'm scared. I don't want to go back into a divorce situation, even if it's not my family's divorce. It just brings back so many bad memories and feelings. I don't know that to do.* Her thoughts fell silent as that phrase played over and over again. *I don't know what to do.* In the mist that was her confusion, a verse came to mind in the quiet of the moment. A verse she had memorized with her sister back in college.

Have I not commanded you?
Be strong and courageous.
Do not be frightened,
and do not be dismayed,
for the Lord your God is with you
wherever you go.

"Joshua 1:9," Philippa whispered, comforted by the verse that had led her through so much. *God, I know You are sovereign. I will trust in You to lead me through this. I will trust in You to see me through whatever may come.* With her prayer at a close, a sense of calm came over her. She would be fine. It didn't matter if she got the job or not. God would provide the family with the best person to lead them through it, and if that person was her, then she knew He would strengthen her through the trials.

Philippa rose from the ground and grabbed her phone from the cheap coffee table. She had bought the table from a garage sale and had painted it white; occasionally, she drew little flowers on it with the paint markers her mother had bought her three Christmases ago. She took a deep breath and swiped to call Mrs. White. The phone only rang once before Mrs. White picked up, her voice warm and inviting.

"My, Ms. Philippa, to what do I owe the pleasure of hearing from you this evening? Do you want to come over for supper? Calvin is asleep on the couch, but I'm sure he would wake up to make you his world-famous hamburgers!"

Calvin was Mr. White, but his casual laid back countenance had long ago discarded last name formalities. He was a sweet old man, but his burgers were not world famous because they were good. He had an interesting skill of catching the meat on fire but keeping the inside completely raw. So far, no one had the heart to tell him his food was inedible. "I'm afraid not tonight. I actually called to talk to you about the Johnsons."

"Oh?"

"Yes, are you still willing to get in contact with Mrs. Johnson for me? Or if you would give me a way to contact her myself, that would be great."

The old woman hooted on the other end. "I will talk to her immediately. I had hoped you would have a go at it."

Philippa smiled, twisting the edge of her skirt between her fingers. "Thank you so much."

"Of course. Now, since we are on the subject of dinner— "

"Dinner?"

"Yes, you simply must come over for dinner tomorrow night. There is a nice young man who will be joining us tomorrow, and I believe you two would get along splendidly."

Philippa blushed bright pink. "That's very kind of you, but I don't think so." *My life is about to change in all sorts of ways. I can't deal with all of that and dating. And I'm possibly going to go on my missions trip. I can't start a relationship only to make him have to wait for me for a year, possibly more. No. It's better to not risk it at all.*

"Dear, you simply must put yourself out there more! You can't expect to find Prince Charming if you are avoiding him at all costs!"

Philippa squeezed her eyes shut. "Thank you for your concern, but if I am to go to China, then I really should wait until later to fall in love. But thank you for the offer."

Mrs. White sighed but dropped the issue. "If you are certain. It's just as well, I haven't invited him yet."

Philippa laughed. "You really are conniving. Thank you for all your assistance. It was nice talking to you. I'll see you on Thursday?"

"Yes, dear. See you then."

The phone vibrated in Philippa's hand, signaling the end of the call. She smiled down at her phone. *I should tell Teressa.* Swiping to her sister's contact, her thumb hovered over the contact photo. The picture was from last Fourth of July. Teressa had been dressed in white, but she was covered in explosions of red and blue from their paint balloon fight. The two sisters shared their mother's button nose and their father's almond shaped eyes, but Teressa was the beauty with her thick wavy hair that had come from their mother's side. The sisters were close, so every phone call was an undoubtedly long conversation.

I'm going to need a large cup of tea for this. She put her phone down with a light tap, turning to the kitchen. Her kitchen was small, one of the downsides to the apartment, but she had enjoyed playing around with the space to find new places to put her kitchen gadgets. Her white wooden cabinets matched her fridge and stove in their simplicity. *One of these days, I'm going to put ribbons or something on the cabinet doors. Anything to make this kitchen look a little less sterile.* She wrapped her fingers around the small wooden knob embedded into the wall, the ironing board falling out of the wall compartment. Under the small board hung tons of tiny tea bags, hanging by the intertwined wire boning of the board. Philippa fluttered her fingers through the bags, stopping at the blueberry pack. Philippa grinned at the small treat and lightly pulled it from its binding. She would never admit it to anyone, but she was proud of the use of her ironing board. Philippa didn't own an iron and instead steamed her clothes. The ironing board was pretty much useless to her, but now it was a fun way to hide her tea from the mice that always came at least once every winter.

She immediately got to work heating the water in her red metal kettle. Rather than pull out one of her soup mugs from above the fridge and risk needing to later make more tea, Philippa pulled out her favorite tea pot and cup. The pot was creme colored with pink accents and a large butterfly beside the verse that had been printed upon it.

All things are possible for

the one who believes.

Mark 9:23

The tea pot had a matching mug with the same butterfly and verse. It had been a gift from Charice at Christmas. Philippa could vaguely remember her friend chatting about how, though it was called a tea pot, it could easily hold coffee. Philippa chuckled at the memory. Her stroll through memory lane was cut short by the scream of the kettle. Philippa quickly removed it from the heat and turned off the stove. It was only a few minutes later that the tea was ready, the pot heavy with its delightful contents. Philippa deeply inhaled the heavenly scent as she set her things on the table. She filled her cup and pulled her phone to her ear as it rang.

"Pip!"

Philippa smiled at the old nickname. "Hi, 'Ressa."

"You called at the perfect time. I just got home and have been hit with a burst of laziness, so I haven't left the car yet."

"That sounds about right."

"I thought you would say that. Is this about the Fourth of July? I still plan on coming up, but I refuse to bring the water guns until you promise to fight fair!"

"Fight fair?! I won fair and square. You're just a sore loser."

"Am not! I know you cheated!"

"And how would I do that?"

"I'm not sure yet. But I will find out!"

Philippa laughed, leaning back in her chair as the usual banter calmed her better than the tea. "It will be rather hard to find out when there is nothing to find out." She sipped her tea before continuing, "I actually didn't call to talk about the Fourth of July."

"Oh? Are you going through teacher burnout? I've heard about that happening to teachers, but I didn't think it would happen yet since you only just finished your second year. Congrats, by the way."

"Thank you. And no, I haven't reached teacher burnout. Quite the opposite."

"Did you receive your acceptance letter already?!"

Philippa chuckled, taking a long sip of her tea. "Maybe."

"Maybe?! Philippa Rose Carol, you tell me this instant or I'm going to force you to play Monopoly with me next New Years'!"

"Calm down. I have been accepted into the missions program" Philippa paused, waiting for her sister to finish squealing. "I even have started the process of getting a job this summer so I can hopefully pay for it."

"Oh, this is so exciting. I need victory cake immediately. Do you think I could eat Halo-halo at this hour before eating dinner?"

"Don't you dare!" Philippa's older sister's instincts came and swarmed her. "You know sweets are better after dinner."

"No, they're not. My stomach has more room now so there's more room for dessert! I can't waste room with boring things like salad."

"You are such a sugar nut. Anyways, the job that I have lined up is this babysitting job— "

"There is no way babysitting will get you enough money," Teressa interrupted. Philippa rolled her eyes. Teressa had always been impatient, and the idea of doing something without progressing toward a big goal was something she would never even think about

"You didn't even let me finish talking."

"Don't waste your time with a cheap side job. Give me a week and I can get you an analyst job, or something else like that. The hospital is paying well and probably better than babysitting." Teressa was the child Philippa's parents dreamed of. She had finished high school early and was well on her way to becoming a brain surgeon. She had connections to the big fancy hospital near her university so it truly wouldn't be hard to find a job opportunity. But Philippa was happy in her community, and of course there were the Johnson kids. They needed someone to watch them.

"That's sweet, but I'm going to try finding a job here first. The family I could be working for is supposedly loaded, so the pay should be sufficient. But that's not the reason I'm trying to help them." Philippa paused, taking a sip of her second cup of tea, the heat of the drink warming her cold hands. "The family is going through a divorce. There are two kids, and one of them was my student this past year."

"Oh," the usually talkative girl fell silent. After a few moments, she continued, her voice quiet and slow. "Is that really a good idea? I know you want to help them, but won't it be too much?"

Teressa hadn't had that hard of a time through the divorce. For the most part, it was all she had ever known. But she knew how hard it had affected Philippa. Philippa's heart warmed at her concern, but the reasons it could be hard tilted everything back into the cold gray of her mind. It would be hard to see the family figure out child custody as well as the housing situation. The fighting would be hard. But most of all, it would be hard to see how it all affected the kids. Philippa pushed the thoughts aside. *But that's why I have to do it. I can give these kids the hope that I didn't have back then. I know what's happening, which means I can strategize for it. God can use me to aid them in healing.* "I'll be fine, but thank you."

"If you're certain." Philippa knew there was more, but Teressa held her silence.

"Let's move onto a happier subject. Have you finally caught the attention of that classmate you've been smitten with since last fall?"

"Pip," Teressa whined. "Don't call it smitten. You sound like grandpa."

"Why are you avoiding the question?"

"Okay, okay. I might have sat next to him during class on Tuesday!" Her squeals pierced Philippa's ears through the small phone. "And now we're going to be in the same study group! I'll see him tomorrow night in the library!"

"With a chaperone!"

"It's a study group. Keyword group! There will be enough people there to keep it proper."

Philippa smiled, her shoulders loosening as she got comfy for what was likely to be a long chat.

CHAPTER FOUR

The sun was hot as it beat against Henry's back, but he didn't care. He placed his hands gently into the soft dirt, cupping them under the roots of the plant he had just pulled. He lifted up, taking the weight of the plant as he placed it into the orange clay pot beside him. A bird sang in one of the surrounding trees, and he breathed in the air that was filled with the earthy scent of the plants he had been potting. *Paradise.*

But all good things had to end as the bird's song was interrupted by the shrill Bath Man tune he had made his ringtone. *Who is calling at this hour?* He flipped open his phone, noting the time was seven a.m. and seeing his sister's familiar face above the answer call button. He sighed and slid his finger to answer the call.

"Hi, Angie. What can I do for you?"

"Henry, Jackie just quit," his sister sighed, as she always seemed to these days.

"Who's Jackie?" He wedged the phone between his ear and shoulder as he continued his work. Even though Angela rarely called, he was going to be late if he didn't finish this order.

"Jackie was the kids' babysitter."

"Why did she quit?"

"Some silly excuse. I don't know what I'm going to do! I have to find someone to watch the kids while Horrace and I are at work."

Henry rolled his eyes at Horrace's name. Horrace wasn't the worst brother-in-law. He actually liked him quite a bit, but over the years Horrace and Angela had become different people. Angrier people. *I know divorce isn't biblical but maybe once they're finally free of each other Angie will be like she used to be.* Still, he did feel sorry for the kids. Charlie and Annie were great kids, and it was going to be hard to go through this. *But Annie and Charlie are such hyper happy kids. They'll be fine.* "Just put out an ad in the newspaper."

"Well, I was actually hoping you could come early this year and watch them."

Henry froze. "What?"

"I know you usually come in July, but couldn't you swing it? I'll pay you."

Henry sat back from his kneeling position and took the phone into his hand. He swiped quickly to his calendar. *Maybe if there's only a couple of projects, I can get this to work.* But his calendar was flooded with colors of all the things he had to do. "I'm sorry, Angie. I can rearrange some things but the earliest I could come is the last week of June."

Angela sighed. "That's okay. I understand. I just wish things weren't so unstable here, and Annie and Charlie already know you, so I was hoping the transition would be easier."

Henry sighed as he looked down at his dirt-covered hands. "I'm sorry. But maybe there's someone at your church who could help. The kids know them, right?"

"I suppose," Angela said, her voice dead. "Actually, Gwen was just telling me about some teacher who was looking for work. Maybe she'll do."

An image of an old lady with gray hair and glasses with a cat sweater came to mind. He doubted this was what the teacher would look like, but he still liked the cat sweater enough to smile and count it as a probability. "Well, there you go."

Angela sighed. "I guess so. I just wish this was all easier. But it's hard to live under the same roof as that man."

"Then why don't you move out and begin the split custody early? Didn't you guys already decide on fifty-fifty anyways?"

"Yes, but we would like to keep our image intact. It's good for the kids, and it helps keep the gossips away. But that's a problem for another day. I better let you go. I have to go to work. Horrace is watching the kids today, so *that* should be interesting." Her tone indicated the opposite.

"Have a good day, Angie. I'm praying for you, okay?"

"Thanks. Bye."

The line went dead, and Henry put his phone into his back pocket. But the conversation weighed down upon him as he continued his potting. *Lord, please be with Angela, Horrace, and the kids. Please fill them with your peace during this time. And I pray for this teacher as well. Please give her guidance with the kids and help them all to come to you in repentance. Please help them to rest in you.*

With his prayer closed, Henry was able to better focus on his work, letting the familiar motions of the job take over as his thoughts wandered toward this possible new babysitter.

Chapter Five

Philippa looked down at her hands folded in her lap. She sat at the dark oak octagonal table in the dining room that Mrs. Johnson had pointed to when she had first arrived. Mrs. White had accompanied Philippa to make the introductions, but Mrs. White and Mrs. Johnson stayed in the entryway to chat while Philippa sat where she was told. She didn't mind being alone, but she was being swallowed by her own nerves.

The dining room was a cream white with elegant brown painted swirls lining the walls and doorways. A bright, uninteresting modernist chandelier hung from above, watching all the room reflect its light. The dark wood floor waxed with gloss and mopped to perfection shined in the corner of her eye as she searched for some piece of character in the room to keep her mind company. Crisp cloth napkins sat in a metal tray with glass salt and pepper shakers huddled beside them.

Philippa heard the clicking steps of Angela Johnson before she saw her. Long blonde hair that was gripped into a tight bun upon her head matched her spotless light crisp blue scrubs. Mrs. Johnson had a pleasant smile on her face as she entered the room. Philippa stood immediately to greet the woman.

"Hello, I'm Philippa Carol, thank you so much for meeting with me." She held her hand out to shake Mrs. Johnson's.

"Hello Philippa." She shook Philippa's hand but squinted at her. "Have we met before?" She took a seat across the table and Philippa followed her example.

"Yes. I was Charlie's third grade teacher."

Mrs. Johnson smiled, her tense shoulders loosening. "Ah, yes. Now I remember. Charlie loved having you as his teacher. You made it so fun that Horrace was never worried about running a minute or two behind."

I'm fairly certain Horrace is Mr. Johnson. Philippa repeated the name several times in her head as she remembered him from pick-up. "I'm glad that Charlie enjoyed my class. He has a delightful imagination and always comes up with great ideas for the quarterly creative writing contest."

"Yes. Of course." Though Mrs. Johnson was nodding along, the uncertainty in her voice and the unknowing light in her eyes made Philippa suspect she had no clue what the creative writing contest was. Philippa's heart sank. Charlie had won the last two writing contests. He had been so proud when he had been given the certificate. *She must be overworked. How terrible. I should get her some tea.*

"So, from what Gwen has told me, you are interested in watching the kids for us over the summer?" Mrs. Johnson's voice shook

Philippa from her thoughts. Thankfully, Philippa's teacher's smile had been on her face since the very beginning.

"Yes. I was looking for employment over the summer when I heard you all could use some help. While I am able to help throughout this summer, it may be a little more difficult when school starts again. If you still require me at that time, then I will make sure to be there, but the kids might have to wait in my classroom for an hour after the school day."

"That would work. We can talk more about that, though, when the school year starts. This will go a little differently than my last interview with a nanny since I know your skills with kids. I guess my main question is: why do you think you should get this position?"

Philippa paused and pondered the question. "I have been given a small explanation as to what your family is going through. I was a little older than Charlie when my parents divorced, so I have an idea of what you all are going through. I want to help ease your children into this new phase in life because when I went through it, I wish there had been someone to help me through it."

Mrs. Johnson leaned back in her chair and contemplated the answer. It was several moments before she nodded and said, "Yes, I think you will do. I'm afraid Horrace isn't here to properly meet you and help me with this interview, but Horrace and I have talked about it, and you will be communicating with me for pretty much everything. The position is working from seven a.m. until six p.m. every Monday, Wednesday, and Friday. Occasionally, we will need you on a Tuesday or Thursday, but that will only be every once in a while. Horrace doesn't work on weekends so he has the kids then, and I should have Tuesdays and Thursdays off. You will be in charge of meals, the kids' activities, and caring for their needs. Have I scared you off yet?"

Though Mrs. Johnson smiled, Philippa could see the wary look in her eyes. "No, ma'am. I understand that there is a lot to consider when caring for children."

Mrs. Johnson's smile deepened, smile lines on her cheeks becoming more pronounced. "I tend to work twelve to sixteen hour shifts but Horrace always runs straight home after work, so he should be back by six to relieve you of your duties for the day. Any questions?"

"Will I be keeping track of my hours on a paper log, or would you like a digital log so it is easier access and better for record keeping?"

"There is a digital document that I will share with you where you will put the hours and any expenses made. You will be given a two-hundred-dollar budget every week, and that will be for any activities or food you pay for. You will be paid hourly; I have done the math to show what an average week will be." She pulled a folded piece of paper out of her inside coat pocket. Philippa took the paper and almost gasped at the number. *I guess China isn't going to be a problem* she numbly thought.

"This is including the two hundred for the week?"

"No, we will refund you at the end of the week, but we expect receipts."

Philippa nodded. "That makes sense."

"Is the balance suitable?"

"Yes. Are there any activities the kids are already part of that I should know about?"

"No. Charlie usually plays video games and Annie hides in her room. I would like you to get them out more, but my hopes aren't high that they will willingly go."

Philippa, her hands under the table, fiddled with the hem of her dark floral shirt. "I understand. When would you like me to start?"

"Wednesday, if possible."

Philippa smiled, "Wednesday it is then."

Mrs. Johnson gave a sharp nod and rose from her chair. "Come, I will give you a quick tour of the house."

Philippa rose and followed. Mrs. Johnson was swift as she led Philippa through the living room, a completely white creation without a single smudge to be found anywhere. The upstairs were next, but Mrs. Johnson only pointed to the different rooms from the top stair. Philippa did her best to memorize but knew that it would take a few days to remember which room was which. Back down the stairs, Philippa was shown the most beautiful kitchen she had ever seen. Marble counter tops, a large stainless steel double sink, and a huge stainless-steel refrigerator with a matching dish washer beside it. Double glass doors in the corner opened into a pantry the size of Philippa's bedroom. Philippa smiled at the kitchen. Her mother would have loved it.

"You have a beautiful home," Philippa commented as she turned around to get a better look at the kitchen around her.

Mrs. Johnson smiled, placing her hand on the doorway. "Yes, Horrace and I both put a lot of time and money to create a house we were proud to show off. It's going to hurt to give up."

"Your husband is getting the house?"

"Oh no. We are going to sell it and split the profits. Too many memories."

Philippa silently nodded, ignoring the feeling that clawed at her heart. It was the feeling she had been avoiding since last Sunday. Mrs. Johnson turned and led her back to the ornate entry way.

"Let me get the kids so you all can get introduced, and then I'll let you be on your merry way." She went to the base of the stairs and called up, "Annie, Charlie. Come down, please. There is someone I want you to meet."

Philippa wisely stayed in her spot, waiting for Mrs. Johnson and her children to come and bid her farewell. The children came pounding down the steps, rushing to the bottom. The girl, Annie, who looked to be twelve stopped but Charlie, recognizing Philippa, ran and crashed into her in a hug. Mrs. Johnson laughed and led Annie over to Philippa.

"Ms. Carol, what are you doing here?" Charlie asked, his big brown eyes and mop of sandy hair shining in the entryway light.

"Ms. Carol will be in charge of watching the two of you from Wednesday onward."

Annie sneered, her eyes narrowing and eyebrows drawing together. The girl was the spitting image of her mother with her blond hair and green eyes, though she was wearing denim shorts and a green ogre hoodie. Mrs. Johnson sent her daughter *the look* and turned back smiling at Philippa.

Philippa gave her brightest smile to the girl as she lightly put her hand on top of Charlie's head. "Hello. Charlie and I have met but I haven't had the pleasure yet, Annie." Annie stared motionlessly at Philippa. "Charlie knows me as Ms. Carol but you both may call me Philippa, or Pip if that's easier. My name isn't known for being the easiest to pronounce." Still no response.

"Yes, well, I am sure you have places to be," Mrs. Johnson said, lightly pulling Charlie away. "We will see you on Wednesday at seven."

Philippa nodded and kept her teacher's smile in place. "It was a pleasure to meet you all. Have a good rest of your day."

Philippa smiled at each of them then turned and went through the entry door. Once the door closed Philippa closed her eyes and let her smile fall. *This is going to be harder than I thought if Mrs. Johnson thinks that I will struggle with even getting them out of the house. And Annie already doesn't like me!* Her heart sank, but she tried to reason out of the fear of what was to come. *Mrs. Johnson was kind. And the pay will be enough for me to reach my goal by September.* Still, she dreaded Wednesday. *God, please lead me through this. I know that Annie is simply hurting, and I shouldn't take it as a bad omen.*

"Dear, you really shouldn't daydream in front of their door."

Philippa pealed her eyes open to find Mrs. White waiting for her in the driveway. Philippa shook away her concerns and rushed over to the older woman who looked a little like a weed in her all-green apparel.

"Mrs. White, you didn't have to wait. I had assumed you'd left a long time ago. I'm sorry, if I had known I would have rushed out sooner." Philippa self-consciously pulled a stray hair behind her ear, her fingers brushing the edges of her glasses.

Mrs. White chuckled as she walked the rest of the distance to stroll beside Philippa as they made their way to their cars. "Don't be silly. You and I both know that I could never leave without hearing every detail about how it went."

Philippa let out a strangled chuckle. "Yes, that seems about right."

Mrs. White paused, turning her complete attention to Philippa. "Are you alright, dear?"

"Of course, why wouldn't I be?"

"Why don't we go get some coffee and talk it over."

Philippa contemplated rejecting the idea but paused. She was still confused, and it could help to talk it through. So, she meekly nodded. "Yes, that sounds like a good idea."

Mrs. White clapped her hands. "Then we had better hurry. I am parched. And starved. We'll go to Linda's so I can indulge in my terrible habit of eating three of her scones within a half hour."

Philippa laughed, waiting to make sure that the older woman got into her car in one piece. Philippa hopped into her little red buggy and stared at the steering wheel for a moment. *God, I need your wisdom and peace.* With that small prayer, she began her journey to the coffee shop.

CHAPTER SIX

The door dinged as Philippa entered and held the door open for Mrs. White. The strong aroma of coffee grounds and syrup flavorings overwhelmed Philippa's senses, giving her a small headache. During Spring break, she had become immune to headaches from the overwhelming smells because of how many times she and Charice had come, but that had been months ago. The smells were now just as dangerous as they had always been. Philippa held back her groan of defeat. *I need to just come here a few times every week so I can build up immunity. Everyone in the community loves this place, so I need to be better prepared for when I am next invited to go for coffee.*

Mrs. White got in line, looking at the chalk wall beside her that showed the menu and cute little drawings of mugs. Philippa stood directly behind her, knowing already what she would order. Her order was simple, a strawberry tea with a splash of lemon. It was one of three items on the menu that were not coffee based.

With their orders made, the two went over to one of the small tables right under the shelves on the wall that were filled with plants. The simple wooden tables glowed in the burning light of the sun that eagerly poured in through the window. Philippa took the cold black metal chair, leaving the blue cotton cushioned bench attached to the wall for Mrs. White.

Mrs. White took a sip of her caramel macchiato, then gave her full attention to Philippa, her blue eyes striking. "Now, dear, tell me what is going on?"

Philippa adjusted her glasses as she looked into the depths of her cup, the pink liquid reflecting her silhouette. "You know I come from a divorce family."

Mrs. White pursed her lips "Yes, I recall you telling me about that."

"My parents divorced when I was nine. I don't like to get into it too much, so I'll simply say that I did not enjoy being in a split family. I haven't thought much about any of that in a long time but being around the Johnson's brings back those old ghosts."

"I'm sorry."

"I'm alright. I am long past those days, but I'm worried about this family. I just don't want to mess this up. I don't want to hurt them more than they already are."

Mrs. White lightly tapped the rim of her mug with her thumb. "This is a hard situation to be placed in. But I can say with absolute confidence that you are the best person for the job."

"Oh?" Philippa perked up, intrigued.

"God wouldn't have placed you there if you were not the perfect person for the job. You know better than I do what these kids are going through. And it doesn't hurt that you have already won one of them over. You will have to be careful, but if you are just yourself, you should be fine. You are a very soothing person to be around. And you are very organized. You will provide structure and predictability which will be momentous when their world keeps changing." Philippa smiled. She had always been self-conscious about how mellow she was. She wasn't adventurous like her sister or outgoing like Charice. But the compliment of being a soothing person warmed her. *My blandness may finally prove to be useful.*

"Mrs. White, you and I know you are an extreme gossip."

Mrs. White snorted but nodded. "Yes, I'm afraid the whole state knows."

"But I know you can keep a secret. You've kept my parents' divorce between you and me. I appreciate that."

Mrs. White gave a soft smile. "I knew it mattered to you. It was too personal to share with the world. I may spill the beans about most anything, but I will never share something that the person wants kept between us."

"Well, then I want to ask you about this feeling I've had. But please keep it between us."

"Of course, dear."

"For a reason I can't name, I am terrified of this new job. I don't know why. I decided to do it anyway because I knew that God would use me how He pleases, but still this feeling exists. Why?"

Mrs. White pursed her lips and pondered it. It was several moments before she answered. "Perhaps it is because this family is going through a divorce. Your parents' divorce was hard for you, though you may try to trick yourself and others that it wasn't. This job puts you into the heart of something you've been running from." Philippa paused and considered it. *Maybe. But the divorce was a long time ago. I thought I was over it, but then it comes back at me again.* "I'm sorry," Mrs. White said, interrupting her thoughts. "I should have thought about that before throwing you into the belly of the beast."

"It's fine," Philippa automatically said. She absentmindedly noted that she was wearing her teacher smile. "As you said, God placed me there. We are just going to have to pray. A lot."

Mrs. White grinned and patted Philippa's hand. "Then let us do that right now."

Philippa nodded and bowed her head. Mrs. Whites' voice was smooth and calm, like the surface of a lake in the first hours of the morning. "Dear Heavenly Father, we thank You for your providence in this job for Philippa. Your constant providence is awe worthy. Your love and compassion are evident and amazing in how You have led her this far. We ask for guidance with this next chapter of her life. Lead her in a way that will glorify You and point this family to You. May You shine through her, giving her energy and patience. Please give her peace. Amen."

Philippa took a deep breath, encouraged and ready to tackle this problem with a freshness she hadn't had twenty minutes ago. "Thank you, Mrs. White."

"Of course, dear. Now, let's talk about strategy. What are you going to do with the kids?"

Philippa bit her lip. "I don't know. The house didn't give any clues as to what they do for fun."

"Yes, Angela prides herself on her clean home, but it makes it distinctly hard to see the kids interests without their art on the fridge or toys lying around."

"I was thinking about taking them to the park. Maybe bringing a ball to play with?"

"Good idea. Annie will probably pretend she doesn't like it until she gets caught in the fun."

Philippa refrained from groaning. "It's going to be hard for the first few days because she will hate everything we do until she's more comfortable." She pulled a pen from her dark skirt pocket, smoothing the wrinkles in the flower pattern down with her fingers. Philippa took the slightly tanned napkin from the table and wrote it out.

Park (With ball)

"Maybe we could also go to the museum?"

"The museum?"

"Yeah. They added a new underwater section that the kids might find interesting. Oh! We could go to the city garden! If you pay five dollars you get to keep a plant! It will be a fun way to learn about photosynthesis." Philippa felt true blue excitement as she glowed with her joy.

Mrs. White chuckled. "You are such a teacher."

"I am," Philippa quickly wrote down the two new destination ideas. She could picture it now: the colored glass pathway that opened to the world of green and flowers. Their mellow scent was a comforting memory to Philippa. Even the memory of the less overwhelming scent helped ease the headache that was currently growing as the scent of coffee seemed to expand.

"But what will you do to get them out of the house?"

"Tell them it's time to leave," Philippa answered simply.

"Don't you expect some lashing out?"

"Yes, but I was thinking about the way that Mrs. and Mr. Johnson use a firm tone with them. They give orders and expect immediate obedience. I just need to establish that leader role, and then that respect will transfer over. Hopefully."

Mrs. White nodded in approval. "A sound point."

"Yes, but the problem is trying to keep things more intimate. I don't want things to be so stiff between us. I want them to like me, but more than that, trust me. I want them to know they can talk to me when things inevitably get hard. But I know it's going to take time."

"All the best things do." Philippa nodded, but her mind was miles away with the Johnson children and the family that was breaking apart.

Chapter Seven

Philippa looked in the cheap full-length mirror she kept attached to the inside of her closet door. Normally she wore skirts, but today she had opted for some pants. Her dark blue jeans and light blue shirt with tulips upon it were clean without a single wrinkle, but she still felt odd. *Oh, it's just the nerves.*

For as long as she could remember, Philippa had always loved the morning. She usually rose before the sun and went to work at five-thirty, the earliest the school opened. Getting a fresh start and beginning as soon as possible were how she managed her day. But today was different. Today, she had to sit around her home for hours, waiting for the moment she could go and finally start her day. Her morning had been filled with much Bible reading and prayer. Her nerves were eating her, and she wanted to cry at the lack of something to do. She peeked her head out of her room and looked at the oven. Her muffins still had five minutes to bake.

Philippa glanced at the counter, mulling over the idea of baking one more thing. Philippa shook her head no. It wouldn't do to add another sweet to her small countertop. The counter was already covered in chocolate dipped pretzels, Rice Krispies treats, and cake pops. *At least I'll have something to bring to tomorrow night's prayer service.* Philippa ducked back into her room and checked the bag she planned on bringing with her.

Let's see. I have my first aid kit, a large edition of The Adventures of Winnie the Pooh, my travel set of Uno, and some colored pencils. Philippa checked through her bag again, digging through the items to make sure that her Bible was in there as well. It was the worn brown leather travel Bible she brought with her everywhere, the weight familiar in her hand. She lovingly caressed it, pulling it from her bag. She opened the book to her favorite Psalm.

God is our refuge and strength,

a very present help in trouble.

Therefore, we will not fear though the earth gives way,

though the mountains be moved into the heart of the sea,

though its waters roar and foam,

though the mountains tremble at its swelling,

she whispered, reading the passage aloud in hopes that hearing it would further establish the words in her heart. "Lord, I need your guidance," her prayer began. She paused. She hadn't thought to pray, so the words had startled her, but now that her prayer had begun, she knew it was what she needed. "Please guide me through this day. May your peace be in the house, and may we feel your comfort as I know it will be awkward for all of us to get into a new routine. Please be with us on this day. In Jesus' name, Amen."

Philippa stared at the worn Bible in her hands. The spine was cracking, and the gold shine that used to edge the pages had faded long ago. Her handwriting filled a large portion of the spaces between verses and on the sides of the page. Her Bible was one of the few unorganized things she owned. She had received it as a gift when she was thirteen and had always used whatever pen was near her to write her notes into it. Many times, she thought about getting a new Bible and having it color coded, but she felt that this Bible was too precious to replace, her notes revealing all the growth that she had gone through with it.

Her oven timer snapped her out of her daze. She placed the Bible back into her bag and went into her kitchen to pull the muffins out. She waited three minutes before she pulled one out and ate it as she prepared all her things for the adventure of the day. Philippa took a deep breath and looked at the clock. *Time for the day to begin.*

Philippa stared out at the impressive house in front of her. She was four minutes early, but she didn't think the Johnsons would mind. Philippa placed one foot in front of the other as she made her way up the path, putting her hand out beside her so her fingers could lightly brush against the greenery that bloomed beside the walkway up to their front door. Though the sun was already beating down with the promise of summer heat, the green leaves were cool to the touch. Much too quickly, Philippa made it to the large white front door. Tentatively, Philippa lifted her hand up and knocked on the door.

The door opened to reveal the one family member Philippa had been hoping wouldn't open the door. "Good morning, Mr. Johnson," Philippa lightly bowed her head in respect.

Horrace Johnson was wearing a fine suit, his sandy hair gelled to perfection. He frowned at her, his brown eyes piercing. "Ms. Carol? What are you doing here?"

"Mrs. Johnson hired me to help watch the kids, and she told me to come at seven a.m. on Wednesday."

Mr. Johnson turned, not making any motion to invite her in. "Angela, did you hire Charlie's teacher to watch the kids?"

Philippa could vaguely make out the sound of shuffling before Mrs. Johnson appeared beside her husband. She gave a brief smile to Philippa before turning to Mr. Johnson. "Yes, dear. Remember, I told you yesterday."

"You said you hired someone, not Charlie's teacher."

"What does it matter?!"

"You could have made me more aware that we could possibly have some issues with the school."

"Why would we have issues with the school? Charlie is no longer her student. His new teacher is going to be Gwen." Though Mrs. Johnson's voice was musical, her smile looked more and more forced by the second.

"I see." Mr. Johnson nodded, but he kept making eyes at his wife who was blinking back at him. *Are they speaking some kind of secret language only they know?*

"I apologize, Mr. and Mrs. Johnson, but it is already," she looked down at her small silver watch on her left wrist, "seven o' five. I'm not sure what time you need to be at work, but I would feel awful if you were late because of me."

"Ah, yes," Mrs. Johnson turned back to Philippa. "Thank you for the reminder."

Mr. Johnson looked down at his watch as well and grimaced. "I have to get going." He moved out of the doorway so Philippa could finally enter.

The entryway was a large white marble area with a small book shelve to the side that was painted black, a stark contrast to the rest of the entrance. Philippa sighed in pleasure as she pulled off her shoes and put them next to the others in the cubby. It was funny to her how much joy the shelf gave her. In her home growing up, her family had a small shelf similar to this one. Of course, this one was far more lavish. In her hazy memories, she could see her father at a garage sale buying it. *He had been so excited to show it to Mom.* Philippa turned and faced Mrs. Johnson.

"Come along, let's head to the kitchen." Mrs. Johnson said, leading the way. "The kids are still upstairs. They were getting ready for the day and working on their chores when you got here, but they probably won't come down until breakfast. Since it's summer, they like to take it slow in the mornings."

The kitchen was just as beautiful as when she first visited. The counters glowed from the overhead white lights. The large window behind the sink was shut, the silver blackout curtains drawn. Philippa placed her bag under the counter, her bottle of tea placed atop the glossed marble. With her things in their place, she turned to Mrs. Johnson once again.

"You will want to start making breakfast. I have some freezer meals in the fridge, or a lot of ingredients in the fridge. Lunch is usually eleven thirty, and dinner is at six. If, for any reason, Horrace and I don't get back on time, they need to be in bed by ten."

Philippa blinked in surprise but nodded. She had never even considered the idea that both of them could be running that late.

"There are emergency contacts in the file drawer in the office upstairs. If you need help, one of the children will know where to look." Mrs. Johnson picked up her dark blue backpack that matched her scrubs. "Other than that, you should be all good. Do you have any other questions."

"Are there any food allergies?"

"No, but good question. The only thing that you should consider for meals is that both kids don't like seafood. Besides seafood, anything is on the table. Horrace and I have tried to give them a variety of different meals over the years so they can handle any dish you give them. Any other questions?"

"No, I think that's everything."

"Well, if you think of anything else, just message me." Mrs. Johnson turned to the door. "Have a good day."

"You as well."

And with that, she left the house. Philippa pushed her glasses further up her nose. *Now, time to figure out what to make.*

Philippa opened the window, both the curtains and the glass, letting in a nice breeze of air. The kitchen was alight with wonder as energy seemed to fill the air. She took a moment to breathe in the fresh air. *Thank you, Lord, for the wonders your creation can do to clear my mind.* She smiled and turned into the pantry. The pantry was full, with a rainbow of different packaged ingredients.

Philippa pulled out a few basic ingredients from both the pantry and fridge, looking them over for some way to create a good impression on the kids. *I suppose this isn't the worst challenge I expect to face today. And I like a good problem. I can work with this.* And so, she did. With a lot of creativity and sweat, she had breakfast made and plated, waiting for the Johnson children to arrive.

Chapter Eight

*S*hould I shout for them? Philippa remembered that was how Mrs. Johnson got her kids downstairs, but that was against Philippa's quiet nature. *No, I shall go and get them myself. I can greet them before they get distracted by food.* With her mind made up, Philippa turned to the stairs and made her way to the children's rooms. She had only made one wrong turn before finding the polished oak railing with white wood support beams. The staircase was across from the television and behind the large white cushioned couch. It was beautiful and clean, but a simple swipe of the curtains and it glowed with the sunlight bouncing against its gloss railing and wooden steps. Philippa tentatively put her hand on the railing. She truly didn't want to smudge it, but she also knew she would freak herself out without the constant presence of support. So, she climbed, carefully gliding her fingers across the gloss.

The upstairs was just as it had been the other day. The wooden steps stretched into the second floor, the light from downstairs fading and growing dim. The only view was a hall with three doors on each side. Philippa stepped to the first door on her left. If her memory served correctly, the kid's rooms were on the left wall. Her small knock was answered by Annie swinging the white paned door and leaning against it. At the sight of Philippa her head tilted, and her mouth turned downward. *Ah, unimpressed with me, are we?*

Philippa put on her best smile. "Hi, Annie. You and I met the other day. I'm Philippa, but you may call me Pip if you want."

Annie gave no response, but her door squeaked under the pressure of her leaning against it. Philippa pushed down the desire to gulp. She couldn't show any sign of weakness or else this girl would tear her apart. "Come on downstairs, I made breakfast." Philippa looked through the doorway at the movie posters that lined the walls, the figurines that lined the light wood desk across the room, the figures exact models from some of the superhero movies Charice had shown Philippa.

At the word breakfast, Charlie popped out of the second door on the left. Philippa took a mental note of where their rooms were. Charlie took one look at her, and a huge smile broke out over his face. "Ms. Carol!" he bounced over.

"Hi, Charlie!" Philippa high fived the small boy. She had learned early on in her first year of teaching that kids liked to high five, so she had naturally adopted the habit. "Are you hungry?"

"Yes!" the small boy answered, his eyes glowing with joy.

Philippa chuckled. "Then follow me." Philippa turned to Annie, who still looked unhappy with her being there. "If you two don't eat soon, then all the food will get cold before we even get down there."

"I only eat cereal for breakfast," Annie said, her voice tight.

She's testing me. Mrs. Johnson would have specified that if it were true. Philippa didn't let any of her thoughts show on her face. In her two years of teaching, she'd learned how perceptive kids are. "Well, then you can have cereal for breakfast tomorrow."

"Why can't I have it today?"

"Because I already made you breakfast."

"That's not my fault."

"Be respectful, Annie. You are not going to get hurt by eating something other than cereal for a day. Now come downstairs." Philippa worked hard to keep her voice strong and authoritative while smiling at the girl. *This is not how I wanted today to begin.*

"Fine," she hissed, "But I have to finish dusting my room first."

Before Philippa could respond, Annie slammed the door shut. *Well, that went about as well as it could have.* Philippa pushed down the feeling of losing the battle before it had even truly begun. Together, she and Charlie went down the stairs, Charlie talking in a rush about the house, giving her a tour as they went down, though his tour was much different than Mrs. Johnson's had been.

"These stairs are perfect for sliding down. Momma gets this fancy stuff to make it shiny. The shinier it is, the faster the slide!" He paused on the bottom step, his eyes wide in bewilderment. "Ms. Carol?"

Philippa looked around to figure out what he was puzzled about but couldn't see anything amiss. "Yes?"

"Why are the curtains open? The curtains are never open. Momma says that it distracts people."

Philippa pinched her lips together as she searched around for a good answer. "I opened the curtains because the sunlight helps me to feel more awake. Even the room is more awake. You see the couch?" Philippa pointed at the couch and waited for his nod. "The couch is smiling now. Can't you tell?"

Charlie tilted his head and squinted at the cushions. His concentration took the form of joy, and he laughed. "Yeah! I do see the couch smiling. I never saw the couch smile before."

Philippa laughed as well. "Everything can smile. You just have to look for it."

Philippa took a step toward the kitchen but paused when she heard the small light thud of human feet. She turned around and froze as Annie came down the stairs. The young girl had her hair down in pin straight locks that draped around her black superhero T-shirt. Her denim shorts were baggy, and it took Philippa a moment to figure out that the random spots of light were little costume jewelry crystals embedded in the pants. The jewels reflected the sunlight, giving tiny rainbows of refracted light across the room. Philippa smiled.

"Hi, Annie."

Annie, done with the non-response strategy, gave a small nod, though she still refused to smile. Philippa wanted to squeal. *Annie responded! Yes, it was just a nod, but that is still something!* Philippa practically skipped as she let Charlie lead her into the kitchen. In the kitchen, Annie and Charlie paused and blinked at the plates. Philippa's heart sank. *I must have made it wrong.*

"You made pancakes?" Annie asked.

Philippa slowly nodded. "I noticed how the pantry is full of just boxed meals, so I decided to make some pancakes. Each of you also got one chocolate chip pancake as well."

Charlie jumped up and down and sprinted to the counter edge where four silver stools rested under the edge of the counter. Charlie pulled out a stool and sat, immediately digging in. Philippa was so startled that all she could do was stand and watch in absolute bewilderment. She had assumed that the kids dreaded the food she made, but right before her eyes Annie pulled out a stool and also began eating the food, a small smile on her lips after the first bite. Philippa approached the counter and pulled out a stool to sit with them.

The two were halfway through their first pancake when Philippa remembered the most important part of any meal. "Goodness, I'm sorry. I forgot to pray!"

The two kids looked at her, still chewing on their food. "What?" Annie finally said.

"I forgot to pray for the food." Still the children looked confused. *Do they not pray for their food?* The idea hadn't occurred to her. "Here. Fold your hands like this," she put hands together, her fingers entwined together, to show them. "Then close your eyes. We do this to keep from getting distracted. And then bow your head. Bowing your head isn't necessary, but it's a sign of respect to God and honors and glorifies Him."

"Why do we have to honor Him? He's not real." Annie shifted in her seat so she could better face Philippa.

"Yeah, Momma and Dad only pray on Sundays in the church. They say that's where you're supposed to pray," Charlie added, his voice going up at the end as if it were more of a question than a statement.

Philippa paused, unsure of how to answer. She didn't want to contradict the Johnson parents, but she also didn't want to stop giving thanksgiving to God for the food. *Lord, please give me the words. I clearly need to study my Bible more, so I'm better prepared for these kinds of moments, but for now, guide my answer and don't let my words stumble the family away from You.* "That is how your parents feel, and I respect that, but since I'm watching you while they are away, we're going to give thanks."

"Thanks, Ms. Carol," Charlie said.

"Oh, you're welcome. But I was referring to thanking God for the food, but I deeply appreciate your thanks." Charlie nodded, a wide smile creasing his cheeks. "Okay, so if you will bow your head and close your eyes, we will begin." Charlie did so immediately but Annie made no motion to follow. Philippa stared at the girl unflinchingly. Annie glared at Philippa, but Philippa held her peace, staring into the girl's lovely green eyes. Annie sneered at her but finally bowed her head, though she kept her eyes open. *That is fine. It's better than I thought it would be.*

"Dear Heavenly Father, we thank You for this food You have provided us. I pray that You will be with us this day and that we will glorify You, Lord. In Jesus' name, Amen."

Philippa barely opened her eyes to find the kids back to eating their pancakes. Philippa smiled.

"Ms. Carol?"

"Yes, Charlie?"

"Did you make these homemade?"

"Sort of."

Charlie hummed in delight. "Usually, we just have cereal or whatever's premade in the fridge. The last time we had pancakes was on Annie's birthday. Remember Annie?"

"No," the girl muttered.

"Sure, you do. We went to that pancake restaurant, and Mom and Dad gave you that weird necklace. The one with the leaf."

"It was a four-leaf clover."

"See! I told you that you remembered." Charlie lifted his chin in triumph, but Philippa studied Annie. The girl had seemed defensive of the necklace and yet uncaring about the day she got it. *Something must have happened.*

Philippa thought through what Charlie had said. *Wait, they haven't had pancakes since her birthday?* "Annie, when was your birthday?"

"Why does it matter?" the girl hissed.

"It's in December," Charlie supplied. "I remember because her birthday is after turkey day but before Santa comes."

"Ah," Philippa lightly patted Charlie, the reward for remembering that far back. Annie rolled her eyes but didn't say anything more. "So, I understand that you guys like to stay indoors and do your own kind of thing, but I think it would be fun to go to the park sometime today."

"The park! Yes!" Charlie's enthusiasm made Philippa laugh but had no effect on Annie's sour mood.

"You guys can go. I just want to stay home."

Philippa immediately shook her head. "No. I am going to let you and your brother do your electronic activities for the next hour and then we are going to the park."

"You can't make me go," Annie huffed.

"Annie, your parents left me in charge of you and Charlie while they are at work. If you refuse to listen to and respect me, then I'm going to take away your phone." Philippa prayed that the girl's weakness was her phone. *Why did I say that? I don't even know if she has a phone?! Oh, why—*

Her thoughts were caught off by Annie's dramatic outburst. "You can't take my phone! It's mine! If you so much as touch it, then I'm telling Momma and Dad, and they are going to be so angry with you!"

Philippa kept her cool, unafraid of the girl's threats. She was around eighty percent sure that Mr. and Mrs. Johnson wouldn't be cross with her. "Go on then. If you want, we can test your strategy. You can rebel when there isn't anything wrong with going to the park, and then lose your phone while you make yourself miserable. Or you can listen, enjoy your time on your phone for the next hour and join us at the park."

"My parents are going to freak out with you!"

"Then tell them, I'm not afraid. What I am doing isn't wrong like you are thinking. But let's make this a little more fair. I will let you enjoy your electronics and all-around carefree time for an hour, and then we will go to the park for an hour. If, at the one-hour mark you tell me you want to go home, then we will."

Annie pursed her lips together as she thought through what Philippa was suggesting. "Fine. But just be prepared to leave as soon as the hour is over at the park."

Philippa smiled. "I will try."

Charlie sat with his eyes wide as he stared at the two of them. It wasn't until Annie had finished her breakfast and run back to her room that Charlie finally explained the wonder of what had just happened.

"Jackie, the last lady to watch us, always let Annie do whatever she wants." Charlie spun around as Philippa washed the dishes from the morning.

"Oh? So, you guys must have never left the house." Philippa had intended it as a joke, but Charlie gave her a sad nod. "Oh, I'm sorry Charlie. Don't worry. We are going to be going out and about pretty much every day, weather allowing."

Charlie gave a loud "Yes!" before dashing from the room.

Philippa gave a soft laugh as she watched him leave. She turned back to her chores and thought through the morning so far. *They never went anywhere? Not even to the park?* It bothered Philippa that the kids had been left to stew over everything with no chance for distraction. No chance for fun memories. Nothing to look forward to. Her brain flashed back to her sister and her staying home all the time, never able to get away from the constant reminder of loneliness that was her house. She shook away the memory and went back to the task at hand. *This is both going to be better and worse than I had expected.* She thought back to Mrs. Johnson, telling her it would be a struggle to get the two kids out of the house. *But it's only one kid who doesn't want to get out. Charlie is so excited by the idea of going anywhere that, surely, he wanted to go places while Jackie was here. He's just a kid. Kids thrive at the park.* She couldn't comprehend how the other nanny wouldn't take them anywhere.

Lord, please help me. I want to be upset with Jackie, but I know I shouldn't do that. I don't know what was happening. Please help me not to be so quick to judge. Amen.

Philippa was still troubled by the isolation the kids had been put through but chose to set it aside and let God guide her.

Chapter Nine

Philippa slipped her backpack over her shoulders, closing her car door behind her. The sun was beating down upon her, and the heat of the backpack didn't help, but a small breeze made the air breathable. The air was thick with the scent of grass and wood chips, the sounds of kids laughing and screaming with joy filling her ears like a melody. Philippa smiled. Though it had only been less than a week since school had been out, she had missed the sounds of kids playing.

Philippa changed her focus to the two kids who had exited the car and were now standing beside her, looking out at the large green fields before them with a playground amongst a large square of wood chips. The playground was metallic in its base structure, painted a dark green, with brown metal stairs, and a ladder that was made from squiggly lines rather than the usual rungs. There were three slides, all made from thick green plastic. A large wavy piece of thick green plastic had holes in it for the kids to climb but looked more than a little like a moldy slice of Swiss cheese. Swings were just beside the playground, and there were several cement benches that were filled with mothers watching their kids while they socialized.

Annie scrunched her nose in disgust at the sight, but Charlie was shaking in excitement. "Ms. Carol, may I go and play on the playground?"

"Of course. Just stay on the woodchips where I can see you."

Charlie didn't even respond; he just dashed off to go climb the odd green cheese while Philippa and Annie stood beside the car. Philippa turned to Annie. "Don't worry," she told the girl as she went over to her trunk. "I brought something for you and me to do."

Annie, caught by curiosity, followed her. Philippa opened her trunk, revealing all kinds of balls in the back. There was a volley-ball, soccer ball, basketball, softball, and football. Annie raised an eyebrow.

"I figured you wouldn't want to play on the playground, so I packed up some stuff. Go on and pick your poison. I am by no means good at sports, but we should still be able to have fun, even if it's just us laughing at me."

"You're going to play ball with me? Why? Don't you just want to sit on the bench while Charlie and I mess around?"

Philippa looked from the benches of mothers back to Annie. The girl was blank-faced as always, but Philippa didn't miss the way she was shuffling her feet.

"No, I would rather hang out with you. I brought you here, why wouldn't I want to have fun with you?"

Annie's shoulders fell and her face softened, a small upturn barely visible at the corner of her mouth. Philippa's heart warmed at the sight; feeling bold, she lightly touched Annie on the arm. Annie jumped a little at the touch but didn't seem to mind.

"Come on, pick the sport of your choice."

Annie hesitantly pulled the soccer ball out. Philippa laughed in her joy. *I can't believe she's working with me! I thought she would sit by a tree and just wait until it's time to go.*

"Is soccer alright?" Annie asked, already holding the ball close to her.

"Of course. You picked my sister's favorite game. When we were kids, we used to kick it around at my dad's house." Philippa closed her trunk and began the trek over to the field on the other side of the trees.

"Your dad's?" Annie asked, dashing a little to catch up with Philippa.

"Yeah, he had this huge back yard with these two trees that were next to each other. We usually used the space between them as a goal."

"So, your parents were divorced also?"

"Yes." Philippa's shoulders drooped slightly, but she pushed the feelings away. "My parents split when I was nine."

"So, was it better after the split?"

Philippa paused. *How do I phrase my answer? I don't want to make her feel worse, but I also don't want to be dishonest.* "The fighting stopped, so in that way, yes. But I didn't like living in two houses. My little sister, on the other hand, loved it."

"That's the only thing you didn't like? The two houses?"

Philippa sighed. *I'm going to regret this.* "Yes, because I may have lived in two houses, but I never had what I considered a home." Annie froze, so Philippa rushed to say, "At least not until high school."

"What happened in high school? Did your parents get back together?"

"Unfortunately, no. But in freshman year, I began going to this church a friend of mine went to. There was so much love and unity that I needed to know more. I wanted so desperately to understand what was so special about that place. A year later and I was baptized and saving up to become a sort of missionary."

"But I've been to church. I've seen you occasionally play the piano at church for offering. I don't see anything special about that place."

Philippa pursed her lips as she thought through what to say. "Next time I see you at church, I'll take you around, and maybe I can show you what I'm talking about."

"That's not going to happen. We only stay for the sermon, and then we leave."

"I'll figure something out. Now, let's start playing."

Philippa put two large rocks into place as the goal while Annie did the same for her side. The ball in the middle, Annie and Philippa ran to kick the ball. Philippa's foot connected and sent the ball flying, but its momentum stopped as Annie threw her ankle in the way to block it. Philippa sent her foot in a quick kick toward the ball, kicking air as Annie used her heel to tap the ball behind and around her so she could kick it toward Philippa's goal. *Ah, so she's played before. This is going to be harder than I thought.* The two continued playing, Philippa constantly being caught off guard by Annie putting her all into the game. The fun game quickly became serious as Philippa rushed to keep up with Annie's persistence.

The sun was high in the sky when Charlie came to join. It was only a few more minutes before other kids joined in. The game went from two players to nearly thirty. Philippa was huffing and puffing from the large amount of energy the game required of her. She hadn't run around this much since college, and she was feeling it.

But the laughter that surrounded her was intoxicating. *I wish I could freeze this moment and stay within it.* Her lungs, however, had a different plan for her. Philippa coughed twice and went over to the side of the field so that way she could watch the game and take a moment for her breathing to regulate itself. Annie and Charlie didn't even notice. They were too immersed in the game.

Philippa looked at her small watch, squinting to figure out the time. It was nearly noon. *Whoops. We've been having so much fun, I completely forgot about the time.* Philippa waited for Annie to score before she called the children.

"Annie! Charlie! We have to go home for lunch!"

Annie and Charlie looked at the ball, then at the other kids. Philippa walked over to the kids still playing. *I wish I didn't have to take the ball.* She wanted to leave it but knew that she couldn't. *Maybe I can let them play a bit longer?* But Philippa brushed the thought away before it had a chance to take root. The kids needed to eat lunch, and she had already been irresponsible in not getting them home by now.

"Sorry, guys," she told the other children who had been playing with the ball. "But if you come to the park again tomorrow, then I'll bring the ball, and we can play again."

The kids smiled and chattered to each other as they ran back to the playground. Philippa smiled as they raced away, happy to not have to deal with a meltdown.

"Ms. Carol, do we have to leave?" Charlie asked.

"Yes, we have to get some food into that tummy of yours."

"But I'm not hungry!" His timing couldn't have been worse, because once his sentence was over, a loud growl came from his stomach.

Philippa laughed and patted his shoulder. "Come on." She began the trek back to her car. "Did you two have fun?"

"Yeah!" Charlie exclaimed.

"Were you serious about coming again tomorrow?" Annie asked.

Philippa looked over at the girl, seeing the hope and fear in her beautiful green eyes. "Of course," Philippa said softly. "I will never lie to you. The only reason we wouldn't go tomorrow is if something stopped us from going, like a storm. And in that case then I wasn't lying, I was just wrong about what day we would go!"

Annie nodded, holding her silence as they made their way to the car. But Philippa didn't miss the smile the young girl kept trying to hide. Philippa's heart soared. *Thank you, God. I know this joy is only possible because of you.*

Chapter Ten

The rest of the day flew by. Annie, when they had returned home, was back to being her grumpy self, rolling her eyes and shutting herself in her room. Charlie, however, taught Philippa all of his favorite non-electronic games, making her run around the house as the day went by. For some reason, the small boy believed she had never seen a video game and that he needed to ease her into the house with games that were more her speed.

Soon it was time for dinner. Combing through the contents of the fridge and the various frozen sides, Phillipa put together a dinner of sauteed turkey, baked potatoes, and roasted garlic green beans. The chill from the freezer that had stained her bones was replaced with warmth from the steam that smoked from the pan. As the quiches she'd whipped together at the last minute rested, Philippa called up the stairs.

"Wash up, please. It's dinner time!"

Philippa turned back to the kitchen and pulled her quiches out to rest on the wire rack beside the metal stove. Charlie, with a stomping speed, came into the kitchen in a dash. "Dinner!" He joyously squealed.

"Did you wash up?" She smiled down at him.

"Yes, Ms. Carol."

"Fantastic, then come along and help me set the dining table."

"The dining table?" His confusion made Philippa tilt her head in like confusion, but it was Annie's shrill voice made her pause.

"We don't eat in the dining room, and you can't make us!"

"I beg your pardon?" The sudden aggression from Annie froze all of Philippa's thoughts, but her teacher's small smile came up like an auto response.

"We never eat in the dining room unless Momma and Dad bring their friends," Charlie replied.

"We eat dinner in the kitchen." Annie looked in the direction of the dining room, her gaze unfocused, but her frown etched in stone. Philippa tentatively stepped over to her. *This is odd behavior. She wasn't even this upset about going to the park. There is something wrong.* Philippa lightly touched Annie's shoulder, the girl's cotton shirt soft upon Philippa's fingertips. Annie looked up; her green eyes hard as they focused on Philippa.

"If it matters this much to you, why don't you and your brother help me set the counter." Philippa softly said, her voice a light caress that froze Annie.

"What?"

"I said we will eat in the kitchen tonight." Philippa grabbed two plates from the cupboard to her right, handing them down to each of the kids who took them with a blank expression on both of their faces. "I'm sorry. I didn't realize it mattered to you that much. I will give you better warning next time, so you aren't caught off guard."

Annie and Charlie melted into motion, helping place the plates on the counter as well as utensils. They remained silent, Charlie keeping a constant eye on his sister. Annie was oblivious to the attention on her as she calmly sat down. Charlie hopped up as well, and the troubled look on his face vanished at the sight of the food.

"Where did you find all of this stuff?!" Charlie asked as he leaned in to deeply inhale the scents.

Philippa laughed, "I just used the stuff you guys had in your freezer and spice rack."

"Momma and Dad's food never have this yellow stuff!" Using a fork, he gestured to the small quiches.

"That is true, but you guys had all of the ingredients. Now, I'll just give a quick prayer, and then you both can dig in." Philippa waited for the kids to fold their hands, and Charlie to bow his head, before she began. "Dear Heavenly Father, we thank You for this day that You have given us: the joy of the park, and the fun of getting to know each other. We thank You for the food You have provided for us. May You use it to bless and nourish our bodies. In Jesus' name, Amen."

The second she said 'Amen', Charlie dug into the quiche. Philippa had been nervous about making the dish, but she remembered from her time on lunch duty at the school that Charlie liked the little egg and ham muffins the school offered as a side. The small boy took a bite and gave a loud, piercing "Yum!" before devouring the rest. *I should probably ask Mrs. Johnson to always have eggs on her grocery list.*

Annie remained in silence, a glum air around her, but she ate the food in front of her. "So, Annie," Philippa began, trying to get the girl to inch out of her shell. "Did you used to play soccer?"

Annie shrugged, "When I was in second grade."

Philippa scooched her chair closer. "You must have practiced a lot. You completely whooped me at the park, and I've played with my sister for years."

"Not really. I mean, Dad and I used to kick the ball around a bit before it was time for my piano lessons."

"Dad played soccer?" Charlie asked. "I didn't know he knew what that was!"

Annie's shoulders lowered minutely. "It was a long time ago."

Philippa hurriedly changed to a different course of conversation. "You had piano lessons? Does that mean you know how to play the piano?"

"A little."

"That's so neat! There was a lady at the church I went to in high school who used to play the organ. She tried to teach me the organ, but after a few weeks claimed that she had no idea how I made the music sound so terrible. We opted to give the piano a shot, and that turned out a lot better. We used to practice on the church grand piano after church every week."

"That means you can play the Minecraft song!" Charlie piped in. "Sarah can! She told Harry and I that she had to practice for weeks so she could perform it on a big stage."

Philippa smiled. "How exciting! Sarah invited me to come, but I couldn't, though her parents told me she was fantastic." Philippa didn't explain that each performer was allowed a certain number of people and that Sarah had already hit double the maximum. Philippa's smile turned soft as she remembered how Sarah's mother, a shy woman, apologized profusely for the confusion. The poor woman had been so stressed and overwhelmed as Philippa was only the first person on her long list to sadly uninvite. Feeling bad for her, Philippa had given the woman her freshly brewed cup of tea. It had been sad to let go of the tea she had been looking forward to, but the woman's small smile had been worth it.

"Jacob also got to perform on the stage, but he plays some kind of whistle thingy," Charlie said around a mouth full of garlic herb green beans.

"He plays the flute. And don't talk with your mouth full, we want to have good manners," Philippa said, leaving her memories to transfer to the conversation with ease. It wasn't always easy, but having taught third grade for two years, she had become used to switching her focus quickly.

"Is Jacob the one that put his flute in bubble solution for the talent show?" Annie asked.

Yes! She's joining in, and I don't have to drag the responses out of her! It was a small win, but a win was a win. "Yea," Charlie responded. "He had practiced this tune for weeks, and then on the day of the show, his brother had talked him into putting bubble solution into the flute." Philippa giggled at the memory of hearing how terribly the plan had turned out. The bubble solution had coated the inside, which muffled the instrument. Rather than bubbles coming out, the instrument was in a constant state of leaking. "I heard it was quite the show," quipped Philippa.

Annie gave an airy laugh, the sound barely distinguishable. "Yeah, but nothing was better than the kid who had decided to try and pull a chair out of a bunny for his magic trick."

Philippa grimaced at the memory of when the account was shared with her.

"What about the girl who tried singing opera and couldn't break the wine glass, so she threw it across the room?" Charlie giggled uncontrollably.

Philippa leaned back as the conversation filled the room, finding peace in the moment. The peace stayed with her through the rest of the night, from washing dishes, to greeting Mr. Johnson upon his arrival, and on her drive back home to her tiny apartment. The only thought that kept replaying through her mind was the small prayer, *Thank you, God.*

Chapter Eleven

Philippa sat at the small metal table outside Linda's coffee shop, her cup of iced tea dripping with condensation from the heat of the sun. The day was hot, as every day had been since summer had begun, the sun beaming down and reflecting off the pale concrete pavement where Philippa's table and others sat. Philippa breathed in the light floral scent of her matcha lavender tea, the quiet simple moment soothing her.

"Girl, that looks like you got liquid grass, but I like the purple. You really should learn about the finer things in life, namely coffee," a loud feminine voice said from behind her.

Philippa turned around and smiled at who she had been waiting for. "Good morning, Charice."

"Good morning? It's only a good morning after my second cup of coffee," Charice said as she plopped into the metal chair across from Philippa.

Charice was wearing bright red cotton pants that flowed around her and a deep orange shirt that matched the scarf she had tied to hold back her massive curly hair.

Charice took a sip of her coffee and hummed in joy. "Oh, His mercies are new every morning!"

Philippa giggled, "Indeed they are."

"Ah, the nectar that brings me life! It makes being out here almost bearable. I should have worn sunglasses or something; the sun is way too bright."

"Sunglasses would have been smart. I wish I had thought of bringing some as well."

Charice pointed and scrunched her nose, "You don't need sunglasses! You had the intelligence to wear a sun hat!"

Philippa self-consciously adjusted the floppy brim of her hat, the woven straw simultaneously smooth and textured against her skin. The hat was a pale tan with a light pink ribbon that ended in a bow that draped its ends into her hair. Philippa had been worried that morning that it would be too attention grabbing, but she had chosen to wear it because she loved the flowers that sat where the brim met the base of her hat.

"Don't worry, it looks lovely on you," Charice wiped Philippa's fidgeting hands away from the hat. "It both suits your beauty and keeps the sun out of your eyes. A fantastic boon to you. Where did you get it? Do you remember if they had a Coffeeholic themed one?"

Philippa took a drink of her matcha tea, the ice cooling her from the scorching heat. "I believe I bought it at the farmers' market.

There was a whole stall of hats, but I'm afraid I didn't see one that was coffee themed."

Charice sighed. "I suppose that's a good thing. Wouldn't do to give people a warning about my chaos. It's much more enjoyable to catch them off guard."

Philippa laughed, "Aw, but don't you want to share the 'coffee is elite' cause?"

"Yes, but I'm getting a t-shirt for that." Charice put her coffee cup down onto the table, finally taking her hands off the precious drink. "Now, as much as I enjoy talking about how coffee is the best drink, I am far too curious about how your first week was."

Philippa pulled her hair behind her ear. She was itching to pull it back into a bun, but she denied the urge. "It was a lot better than I was expecting."

"How so?"

"Mrs. Johnson had made it sound like the kids would never willingly leave the house, but I only really had problems with that the first day, and only with the older girl. We have gone to the park for the past two mornings so far, and yesterday I packed lunch so we could just eat there and continue playing."

"That's fun. I remember I used to play princesses and dragons with the other kids when I was a kid."

"Is that the one where a knight has to fight a dragon to rescue the princess?"

"You got it. I was always the dragon because I had the loudest roar," Charice sat taller, her smugness rolling off her in tsunami waves.

"That sounds about right. Well, we have been playing soccer. It's been really fun. Usually, a bunch of other kids join in. It's the only time Annie, Charlie's older sister, is completely out of her shell. She laughs and squeals when playing the game, but once out of the game, she is quiet and occasionally attitudinal - nothing too bad. "

"Hmm. That must be hard. If she's any good, maybe you should bring her to tryouts in a few weeks."

"That sounds like a good idea. It would give her some more consistency, and she'd probably make some friends. Soccer is the only thing that's been making her excited lately." Philippa smiled softly at the memories of the week. "Oh, but she is a little weird about the dining room."

"The dining room?"

"Yes, she usually snaps at me and talks back when she doesn't want to do anything; but when it comes to eating in the dining room, her eyes get unfocused, and she gets stuck in this quiet sadness."

"Sounds like it's more than the dining room."

"That's what I'm thinking too."

"Why don't you try to do something fun in the dining room so it's not so stiff? Unless you think that would be more detrimental."

Philippa considered the idea. "I will give it a shot and see what happens. I just want to help her get out of this rut with the dining room."

"I will pray for you."

Philippa's heart warmed. "Thank you, I definitely need all of the prayers that you can spare. Yesterday was pretty good though. We have all fallen into a sort of pattern. Annie doesn't like me, but they both respect me, which is more than I was hoping for."

Charice smiled and lightly patted her hand. "I'm happy that this has been going better than planned. Have you accepted the teaching abroad position yet?"

Phillipa shifted in her chair. "I typed out my response, accepting the position, but I'm not going to submit it until I have the amount ready."

Charice rolled her big brown eyes, her smile goofy and teasing. "You are way too honorable. You can pretty much guarantee that you will have the money."

"Yes, but who knows what will happen between now and then? It's better to not take the chance that things could go wrong."

"I suppose, but is there any other reason you haven't accepted yet?"

Philippa, holding her tea up for a drink, froze. The scent of the tea was strong and tantalizing, but Philippa put her cup down slowly. *How do I explain my reasoning? This is Charice. She's never been afraid of change. How do I tell her that I am a chicken and don't want to lose everyone? She would probably just tell me that I'll always have a place here. While that is true, if I leave it will never be the same.* Philippa cut the thought, slicing it into a million shattered pieces.

"I guess I just keep psyching myself out."

"How so?"

"I don't really know. Every time I go to send in my acceptance letter, I just talk myself out of it. But all of my excuses sound weak."

"Hmm. Well, that at least gives you something to think about. If you want, the next time you go to send in your acceptance and talk yourself out of it, you can call me, and we can talk it through." Philippa relaxed her shoulders; the only sign of relief she would give. *It's not a bad idea. It's probably the best solution. Besides I can't let fear run my life.* "That would be nice, thank you. But enough about me. Tell me, how are things going in the analyst world?"

Charice groaned, sagging further into her chair. "This week I have been working with a pharmaceutical business that wants to adjust their marketing and sales strategy, but they do not like the statistics that I have found after going through *all* of their records."

"I assume the statistics are not in their favor."

"Of course not! And looking at their product and how they package, advertise, and suggest it, there is no wonder why they have so many problems! And Mr. Johnson is also part of the project, and he is not happy that I'm having them rework the product."

"Mr. Johnson is part of the project?"

"Hm? Oh, yes. I didn't even know he worked for this company, but then apparently the problems I have with the product are connected to his unit."

"Oh? I didn't know you worked with Mr. Johnson."

"Because I didn't until this past week." Charice lifted her cup only to frown at its empty contents. Going into her large bag, she unearthed a second cup of coffee, exactly like the last. "Philippa, I have gone through four bags of my Organic Tolima Colombian coffee the past two weeks because of them! Even *I* think that's a lot!"

Philippa smiled softly and lightly patted her friend's hand. *So Mr. Johnson is stressed at work. Maybe that's why he seems a little put out every time he comes back from work.* "Is there any way I can help ease your burden?"

Charice bolted upright in her chair, an evil light shining in her dark brown eyes. "Yes. There is this book called *I Am Texas.* It's rather large. I want you to get that book and hit the top of this company's CEO's head. And then I want you to give them your teacher scowl. If you, this sweet and graceful flower, attack them so viciously, I am certain that they will quake in their boots and finally listen to me!"

Philippa didn't even bat an eye at the request. It wasn't the first odd and vicious plan Charice had made. "How long did it take you to come up with this plan?"

"Half an hour. Cordon, the CEO I report to for the project, had told one of his friends that he hates looking at the reports. The reports I have spent way too many days working on! So, I thought, if he doesn't like to look at the books, then he would love getting hit with the books. But I figured the books weren't big enough to knock any sense in him, so I figured out what the biggest book is."

"And my teacher scowl?"

"Your teacher scowl scares kids, and I thought since he was acting like a child, he should be treated like one."

Philippa tilted her head as she contemplated the explanation. "Well, it is a valid plan. I would love to help, but if this book is as big as you say, then there is no way I can carry it."

Charice sighed. "There goes that plan. I guess I'll just keep going with plan H."

"Which plan is that?"

"Finish the project as quickly as possible so I never have to speak to these people again."

Philippa laughed. Though Charice was a wild card, she was also incredibly smart. Charice was a freelance Business Intelligence Analyst. Her job was to go through a company's data and, in Charice's words, tell them all the ways they are failures. Though she always made fun of people, Philippa knew that Charice did a lot more for them than just business. She would help them in their personal life if they let her. Her heart was always focused on those around her, ready to drop everything to help.

Charice, the bright and wild creature, was in an office job. It had always puzzled Philippa. But Charice had two bachelors', in Business and Statistics, and a Masters in Statistics. She had confided in Philippa once that she had been taking college classes in high school, so by nineteen, she already had her associate degree in computer science. She then immediately went back for her statistics degree, and out of boredom she had gotten her Masters in Statistics. It completely boggled Philippa's mind how someone could go through so much schooling by age twenty-three, but that was just Charice.

"So, when do you think this project will be done?"

"If they listen to my presentation on Thursday, and implement my strategic suggestions immediately, I'll be done in two and a half weeks. If they choose to have me go through another round of their productivity and analyze how well the new plan is working, then I will be there for another six weeks."

Philippa winced. "I'm sorry. I know you don't like being on a single project for very long."

"I'll be fine. Even if I have to stay another six weeks, it will all be worth it because that means they are going to listen to my suggestions. The marketing team is probably going to throw hands at me since I am having them go through and rework their marketing strategy. But the numbers don't lie; their efforts currently are useless."

"Sounds aggravating."

"That is a fantastic word for it."

"So, cranky boss and cranky kid. We should switch problems," Philippa smiled into her drink.

"That would be a terrible idea. There isn't enough coffee in the world to guide me through watching those kids, and they wouldn't love me half as much as they love you."

"And I wouldn't be able to stand up to CEOs the way you can."

Charice raised her coffee in a sign of cheers. "So, our problems are our own."

Philippa lifted her cup to meet Charice's. "And we are the best suited to face our problems."

"May God give us strength!"

CHAPTER TWELVE

The sun was beaming down its heat on Philippa and the kids at the park Monday afternoon. Philippa sat in her peach cotton shorts and her blue and white floral shirt. Her legs were folded crisscross on a thin sheet that she and the kids had laid across the grass for their picnic lunch, the prickles of grass poking her legs with a biting strength. Even with the tall leafy green tree above her providing some shade, the sun persisted in broiling the field. Philippa fanned herself with her sun hat as she watched Annie, Charlie, and some of the other kids play tag.

She glanced down at her watch and frowned. *We should get going soon. I don't want to tire them out.* Annie ran past, a large smile on her face as she tagged the kid she had been chasing down. *Or perhaps another hour wouldn't hurt. They're young, they'll be fine.* Philippa leaned on her hands, content to let them run around and have fun for an hour or two more. The park was the only place where Annie was happy, and that troubled Philippa. *It's only been three days. Maybe she just needs to get more used to me being around.* Philippa doubted that was so. *She's going through so much. She still hates the dining room. Her whole world is tilting. She needs something constant. Maybe a tradition? But what sort of tradition?*

A small, rare breeze for the day pulled whisps of Philippa's hair from her bun, the pieces falling into her eyes. The scent of grass fluttering around as she pulled the pencil from her bun, her hair falling in a thick swoosh. A quick twist of her hands and she had refastened her hair, using the red pencil to lock in the bun. Her hair decently pulled back, Philippa put her sun hat back on, blocking out the scorching sun, as she thought through what to do about Annie.

I'll start small. Maybe a game night after dinner, and if it goes well, then we will continue it. Her shoulders lowered minutely in relaxation at the plan, only to raise back up in worry. *But what if this only hurts them more? I must tread carefully.* Philippa rubbed her fingers on her temples, trying to ease the headache that was creeping upon her. *But I can't just leave things the way they are. I am in a battlefield, and unless someone changes something, they are going to be victims of a battle they didn't choose.* An empty sinking feeling filled her. Everything felt like mountains rising against her, her strength dissipated and her loneliness a knife to her scared heart. She bowed her head. *Lord, this battle is overwhelming, please give me strength.* A verse, through God's grace, came to mind.

I love You, O Lord, my strength.

The Lord is my rock and my fortress and my deliverer,

my God, my rock, in whom I take refuge,

my shield, and the horn of my salvation,

my stronghold. Psalm 18:1-2

Philippa inhaled deeply, the air thick with the scent of freshly mowed grass. *God, You are my strength. Teach me to rest in You. I know You are my shield, my rock, and my refuge. Help me to rest in Your plan. I know that I can depend on You to guide me through this. Please give me wisdom, may my words and actions glorify You and lead the kids to grow in You.*

"What are you doing, Ms. Carol?"

Philippa looked up to see Charlie sitting across from her. She smiled at the amount of dirt that covered him from head to toe. *I'll just have to remember to cover my car's back seat with the sheet, so he doesn't get mud everywhere.* "I was praying."

"Praying? Why? You aren't eating, and it's not a Sunday," he ran his fingers through his messy curls that were more brown than blonde due to running around in the dirt so much.

"I love talking to God. The Bible tells us that we are to pray constantly. God wants to hear from us."

Charlie's eyebrows lowered. "He wants to hear from us? Why?"

Philippa grinned at his inquisitive brain, happy that he wasn't just leaving the conversation at that. "He loves us. For those who believe in Him, He wants to have a close relationship. Those who believe in Him are His children, His beloved children. Praying is something so special I try to do it as often as I can, though I will admit I get distracted a lot."

"Distracted by what?"

"Lots of things. Sometimes I start praying, and then I get really hungry, so I go and look all over the place in a gigantic adventure to find chocolate. Or I will be praying and suddenly remember that I forgot to call my sister. And sometimes, when I pray at night, I accidentally fall asleep!"

Charlie giggled. "How can you fall asleep while talking to God?"

"I don't know. I just start praying, and then—" Philippa shut her eyes and fell to her side, beginning to snore loudly and over-dramatically. The performance got her desired reaction: Charlie's high-pitched laugh echoed across the field. Philippa opened her eyes and winked at the small boy. She pushed herself back into her sitting position and made a big motion of shaking away the sleep. "You see?! What did I tell you?"

Charlie's smile dimmed slightly, "Does God get mad at you for sleeping while praying?"

Philippa's smile softened as she inched herself closer to the small boy, her hand closing around his dirt and grime covered fingers. "No, He is loving and forgiving of all my silly little mistakes. I never have to fear, because His love is everlasting; meaning He will love me forever. Does that make sense?"

Charlie tilted his head. "How can His love last forever? Annie says that love is only for a little while, and then it disappears."

Philippa's heart broke at the declaration. "Your sister is hurting and scared, she is confused and lost. She may have given up on love, but you and I are going to prove her wrong. Do you love your sister?"

"Mostly."

Philippa smiled. "I love your sister. And I love you. Do you think that I'm ever going to stop loving you?"

Charlie stared off into the distance. "I don't know."

Such sorrow at such a young age. This is truly a broken world. "Charlie, I promise I will always love you. I love you to the moon and back."

Charlie blinked. "That's far."

Philippa chuckled, and she squeezed his fingers twice. "Yep. That means I love you a lot. And if I love you that much, you can rest in knowing that God's love is more than a billion times bigger than that!" *He may not believe me now, but I am going to shower them both in love until they finally believe me.* "Go on ahead and play around some more, we're going to be leaving in forty-five minutes."

Charlie bobbed a nod and bolted off the blanket, aiming to run back to the kids, but pausing at the edge of the sheet. "Ms. Carol?"

"Yes, Charlie?"

The boy ran at her, nearly knocking her over in his hug. "I love you, too."

Before Philippa could respond, he was running over to his new friends. Her heart felt as though it were soaring as she was filled with every warm feeling that she thought could ever exist. *Thank you, Lord.*

Philippa lifted her hand to wipe away the dirt on her clothes from the hug but stopped. Slowly, she put her hand back in her lap, her mother's prim training out the window. *I just want to hold the mark of this memory a little longer.* And so, Philippa let herself sit in the dirt, her hair messily out of her bun, as she stared out at the view of God's grace.

Dinner came and went with a speed that Philippa wasn't mentally prepared for. Her nerves spun webs upon webs of anxiety as Philippa set the dining room table with games that she had found hidden in one of the hall closets. *I have nothing to be worried about. I warned the kids when we got home that we would be doing something in the dining room after dinner, so they have had enough time to get used to the idea of doing things in here.*

Still, nothing could calm her. *This is nonsense. I wasn't even this anxious when I took my third graders to the zoo, and Harry thought it would be a good idea to throw rocks at the lions to see if they could catch.* Philippa scrunched her eyes shut as she tried in vain to be rid of her worries. *I just don't want to hurt them.*

A creak, small and almost indistinguishable, had Philippa spinning around. Charlie and Annie stood peering at the table that had been flooded with board games. Charlie was bright eyed as always, but Annie was sour faced. *I can take sour.* Philippa gave her teacher's smile as she moved slightly to the side, motioning for them to come the rest of the way in.

"Go ahead and have a seat. I found all sorts of games around the house. I think that taking turns choosing a game to play would be best."

Charlie ran to the table and hopped into a seat. Philippa kept her eyes on Annie. The girl hesitated, her arms crossed over her chest, and her green eyes were narrowed. Philippa found she couldn't breathe as she waited for Annie to make her move, but she kept her teacher's smile on her face, showing no sign of concern or weakness. Annie entered the room and sat next to her brother, but Philippa didn't miss the upturn of her nose at the sight of the games. *Thank you!* Philippa sent the quick prayer before sitting on the other side of Charlie at the octagonal table.

"Charlie, why don't you choose first," Philippa suggested, gesturing to the games she had stacked.

Charlie leaned over onto the tabletop and shuffled through the games, gasping in delight when he had selected one. "Dutch Blitz!"

Philippa looked at the game. It was a small card box with two Dutch children on the front of it. She had never heard of it but had picked it up when she had found it because she assumed that it would be good to have options that even she was unfamiliar with. "Perfect. Do you know how to play it?"

Charlie nodded. "Uncle Henry bought it for us and used to play this with us all the time!"

"We can teach you the rules," Annie added.

Philippa nodded, but on the inside, she was jumping with glee. *A shred of kindness! It's official. Games are the way to her heart!* "Teach away."

Annie and Charlie bumbled over each other as they explained the rules, but it was only after a practice round that Philippa understood how to play. The gist was that you had a small deck of ten cards that you were trying to get rid of, and a large pile of cards in your hand. With the pile of ten, you could only use the top card, but the bigger pile you could run through multiple times. You got rid of cards by putting them in the middle with the other players' cards, but the piles had to count from 1-10. The faster the game went, the more chaotic it got, something Philippa learned quickly. Charlie dominated the second game, flying with the speed of a zipping dragonfly.

The game flew by, and it was only after the fifth round that Philippa paused, catching her breath from the intensity of the game. "I'm sorry Annie, I almost forgot! It's your turn to pick a game."

Annie barely glanced at the pile of games before shrugging. "We can keep playing this one."

"Are you sure?"

"Yeah, I have to beat Charlie or I'm never going to live it down." She flipped her hair over her shoulder, nonchalant.

Philippa laughed. "If you're sure. Let me just sort my cards—"

A loud slam echoed in the house. Philippa's eyebrows lowered in confusion, but Charlie jumped out of his seat in excitement. "Dad's home!"

He ran over to the front door, Philippa close behind. As Charlie had said, Mr. Johnson was standing in the doorway. The neat and clean man from the morning was gone. His hair was a mess, and he was in the middle of violently throwing his shoe into the cubby.

"Dad! Do you want to play Dutch Blitz with us?!" Charlie asked, clearly not reading the frustrated look on Mr. Johnson's face.

"No, what I want is for those idiots in charge to get a clue and fire the lunatic who keeps suggesting we change our entire company!"

Charlie's face fell and he took a step back. "I'm sorry, Dad."

Mr. Johnson's shoulders fell, and his face softened. "No, I'm sorry, Charlie. We'll play some other time, okay?"

Charlie nodded but kept his head low. Mr. Johnson nodded at Philippa and Annie before turning and making his way upstairs. Even though Philippa was officially free to go, she paused and looked at the kids. Both looked like they were puppies that had just been kicked.

She crouched down and opened her arms as an offer to Charlie. Charlie ran into her hug and squeezed tight. Philippa outstretched one of her arms to lightly touch Annie's wrist. Annie pulled back like the touch was fire, scorching her skin. Philippa watched in heartbreak as Annie stumbled away and went over to the stairs. Not a word was spoken, but Philippa felt as though the silence was too loud, a screeching thing that made her overwhelmed and ill.

"I'm sorry, Charlie."

"It's okay," the boy sniffled into her shoulder.

"I love you." Philippa knew that now, more than ever, the boy needed to know he was loved.

Charlie didn't respond, just a small nod. He disentangled from the hug and followed his sister up the stairs. Philippa sighed at the stairs but stood up and pushed herself to go to the dining room to clean up.

I am going to officially make game night every night. They were having a blast before their dad got home. Anger and bitterness rose within her against Mr. Johnson before she took a deep breath. *Lord, please take away my anger and replace it with Your love and kindness. Please work in Mr. Johnson. May You fill him with joy and draw him and his whole family to You. Lord, please work in this broken family and heal them.*

With her prayer finished, Philippa spent the rest of her time cleaning and thinking of the family, wishing she could do anything to help them.

Chapter Thirteen

Philippa was still troubled that Wednesday morning. It was a struggle to pay attention to the road as she drove over to the Johnson's house. She was so distracted that it took her several moments of waiting by the front door, after she had knocked twice, to realize that she could hear yelling. Even though the door muffled the sound, she recognized Mr. and Mrs. Johnson's voices.

They're fighting? The realization struck Philippa. Mr. Johnson had been more and more grouchy, but Philippa had never expected to hear him or Mrs. Johnson's voices raised. Stunned, Philippa stared at the door. *I don't understand; what should I do?* Philippa puzzled at the door when she heard a voice softly call, "They won't hear you."

In surprise, Philippa stepped away from the door and looked around her for the voice. On the second story of the house, sitting on the small balcony, was Annie, her legs dangling down the edge.

"Should I call them?" Philippa asked.

"No. When they get like this, nothing can distract them from getting their point across." Annie stared at her and scooted slightly to the side. "You can boost yourself on the trash can and climb up here."

Philippa looked at the trash can in doubt. It was a sturdy black one, but that didn't mean that Philippa trusted it to hold her weight. *But she shouldn't be alone.* So, Philippa swallowed down her fear and pulled herself onto the can.

"Where's your brother?"

"He's in his room. Probably playing videogames with his headphones on. That's what he usually does when they are talking this loud."

The nonchalant explanation, mixed with the shouting that was still audible, brought Philippa back to when she was a young girl. The never-ending fights, the constant excuses, hiding in her bedroom just waiting for it to end. *But I don't understand. Mr. and Mrs. Johnson are known for being peaceful people. I've never even seen them bicker. How could this not be the first time? How has nobody noticed before?* The dim cloudy morning felt darker and more oppressive, but she pushed away the feelings and memories, pulling herself onto the balcony to sit beside Annie.

From the safety of stability, Philippa studied the view. The brick and wood houses all mirrored each other to the point where Philippa truly couldn't tell one from the other. All neat houses in their own happy corners, but Philippa had to wonder how happy they truly were. Mr. and Mrs. Johnson looked like the picture-perfect duo, but their yelling crackled and tore that perfect picture.

An extremely loud yell made Philippa wince, but Annie just stared out at her neighborhood. The lack of any motion or emotion from Annie brought Philippa's arm around Annie's shoulders. She didn't move or even seem to notice Philippa's touch. *Lord, please give me wisdom. Bring peace to this home. Amen.*

On a whim, Philippa said, "I was nine when my parents got a divorce, but they used to fight like this."

Annie pulled back. The shouting was still there but more muffled and less distracting as Annie wrinkled her nose. "They aren't fighting. They're just having a discussion."

Philippa shook her head. "No, they are fighting. Don't confuse discussion with fighting, or someday you won't be able to tell the difference, and you will bring that habit into your future relationships."

"No, they are just talking things through."

Philippa looked into the young girl's eyes and decided to let it go. "You have a lovely view," she gestured vaguely to the houses and sky that surrounded them.

Annie sighed at the sight. "We used to eat in the dining room."

"Pardon?"

"Momma, Dad, Charlie, and I. We always ate dinner together. Every night. Until two years ago. That's when the fighting began."

Philippa sat in silence, unsure of what to say or do.

Annie didn't notice the state she had thrown Philippa into. She just kept talking. "It was small at first, but then it got louder and louder. I used to be in gymnastics, dance, and art classes all around town, but back in August they both got too busy with their work that they no longer had time to drop me off. Then one day, while we were eating in the dining room, Momma told us that she and dad were getting a divorce."

The dining room... "I'm sorry," Philippa finally found her voice.

Annie shrugged, her gaze unfocused on the clouds that drifted past. "It doesn't matter. I knew that they were going to split when they started hiring babysitters. It used to be that Momma worked the night shift so she could watch us during the day while Dad worked the day shift." Annie sat in silence for a few moments before tears started streaming down her face. "What did we do wrong, Pip?"

"Nothing. You did nothing wrong."

"Then why," her voice broke with a sob, "are they running from us? I keep going through everything that has happened, and I can't understand why they want to stop being a family. Was it because I forgot my homework at home that morning? Was it because I got a B in math? Was it that I'm not as accomplished as some of my classmates? They never fight anywhere but at home. They're always so happy and friendly when others are around, but then we get home.... What did I do wrong?"

Philippa pulled her close and squeezed her tight. "You have to believe me; this is not your fault."

"Then why is our family falling apart? Who's going to tie Dad's tie in the morning? Where are Charlie and I going to live?"

"I don't know why your family is going through this. But I do trust in God to see you through it."

"God?" the girl shrieked. "If there is a God out there, then He is the one putting me through this. He's the one who tore us apart. He is the reason I don't have a family anymore."

"You do have a family. Even after the divorce, your family will still be a family. There are people around who love you, and love is the gift that unites us as family. You are never alone, Annie. I love you, and I've only known you for a week. Imagine how much more your parents love you? I know you don't want to hear this, but there is someone who loves you so much that they died to have you part of their family."

"Who? Why?"

"His name is Jesus, the son of God. You know about sin?"

"Yeah, they teach us about it at church."

"Good. Since sin is our evil that separates us from God, God knew that there was only one way to save us from the punishment of death that we deserve. He sent someone in our place, but not just anyone, His perfect Son who had done no wrong. Jesus died willingly so He could have you as part of His family."

"That makes no sense. He's dead."

"No, He's not, because on the third day, He rose from the grave to bring light and hope to His people. He is now seated beside God in heaven. All you have to do is accept that Jesus is the Son of God, died for your sins because there was nothing to save you besides faith alone, and that He is risen."

"I don't know. It sounds pretty far-fetched."

Philippa smiled softly at the young girl. "Then, why don't you read the book of Mark. It's short and to the point. I even have a spare Bible in my car that you can have if you want."

Annie bit her lip. "How will this give me answers?"

"It might not, but it will give you peace and hope if you choose to believe it. Come, let's go to my car, and I'll get it for you." Philippa began inching herself off the balcony. *I thought getting up here was scary, but nope, this is much worse.*

"Right now?"

"Yeah, your parents are going to finally be able to answer the door now, so there's no reason to wait."

"Open the door? I told you; they can't hear you—" she paused and put her ear against the door that led back into her room. "Oh, they must have realized the time." In a much smoother motion than Philippa, she gracefully hopped down onto the trash can and then to the ground.

Philippa opened her trunk and pulled from one of the side pockets she had Velcroed to the side of the trunk, a small travel size Bible. It was a warm maroon color, and the gold edging on the papers glowed in the sun that was barely peeking through the clouds.

"Why don't you read the first three chapters and then we can talk about it?"

Annie nodded as she took the Bible from Philippa's outstretched hand. She gazed at the Bible with curious scrutiny. At that moment, Mr. Johnson blasted out of the front door. He paused at the sight of her.

"Where have you been? I could be late because of you!" he yelled as he threw his briefcase into his car.

"My apologies sir. I knocked on the door twice over thirty minutes ago, and no one answered. I could hear some things through the door and assumed you two would like privacy, so I sat and talked to your brilliant daughter."

Mr. Johnson had been puffing up in anger until Philippa's remark about Annie. He looked at Annie as though he hadn't realized she was there. *He probably didn't see her. I doubt he would have yelled at me if he had known.*

"Annie, get back inside. Your mother is probably looking for you. I will see you tonight, have a good day." He got into the driver's seat, and with a small burst, his engine started, and he pulled out of the driveway.

Annie's lips were pinched, but she went into the house like her father had told her to. At the doorway, Philippa stopped the young girl. "Annie, I'm here for you. Always."

Annie turned around and gave her a small side hug, "I don't believe you, but the thought still means a lot."

She left Philippa standing in the entryway, frowning at the words and the pain that Philippa knew Annie was going through. *I need to get her some more constants. She needs something to depend on and to be surrounded by more people than just me and her family.* Philippa nodded her head and slipped off her shoes. *What a start to the day.*

Chapter Fourteen

A week had passed and there hadn't been any other yelling incidents. Everything went back to how it had been. After playing at the park, Philippa drove the kids over to the local coffee shop. She bought a muffin for Charlie, and a bacon pepper jack cheese scone for Annie. Philippa was perfectly content with a cup of chai. Chai always tasted like fall to her, so the drink made her feel more festive.

Charlie got himself settled into the kids' corner, where he played with all the toys that the cafe provided, while Annie and Philippa took the lounge seats beside the electric fireplace. The leather cushions on the chairs made Philippa sink into the seat an inch or two while she placed her bag onto the tiled floor beside her.

"Did you read the first three chapters of Mark?" Philippa asked, getting straight to business.

"Yes, though I didn't understand it."

"Well, let's start there. What didn't you understand?"

Annie took a bite of her scone, crumbs falling onto the napkin that laid in her lap as she took her phone out of her pocket. "Why does Jesus have to be baptized? And why by John? John made a big deal about how someone is coming to baptize with the holy water which is presumably better than just water. I thought he was referring to Jesus, but why would He have to be baptized if He is the Son of God?" She flicked her eyes up to Philippa after reading the questions she had typed into her notes app.

Philippa's eyes widened. "Wow, those are great questions, and that's only the first section!"

"Do you not know the answers?"

"Well, I can do my best to answer, but make sure you fact check me later." Philippa waited for Annie to nod before continuing. "So first off, do you know what baptism is?"

"Isn't it what you do to babies to make sure they go to heaven?"

"Not quite. The Bible speaks of three different types of baptism. One is in water, which is a declaration both from the believer and the church that they believe Jesus died for our sins and acknowledgement that salvation is through faith alone. Another is at salvation, where the Spirit baptizes the believer into the body of Christ. And one is Jesus baptizing His people in the Spirit. Now Jesus' was different in that Jesus' baptism was the baptism of John. Acts 19:1-7 shows what the difference is. Why don't we go on and turn to that passage." Philippa opened her Bible and fluttered through the pages until she found it.

"And it happened that while Apollos was at Corinth, Paul passed through the inland country and came to Ephesus. There he found some disciples. [2] And he said to them, "Did you receive the Holy Spirit when you believed?" And they said, "No, we have not even heard that there is a Holy Spirit." [3] And he said, "Into what then were you baptized?" They said, "Into John's baptism." [4] And Paul said, "John baptized with the baptism of repentance, telling the people to believe in the one who was to come after him, that is, Jesus."

Philippa looked up at Annie's confused gaze. She smiled and began to explain further. "John's baptism was a preparation for the Kingdom coming with Jesus' appearance. Jesus was baptized to display and confess alignment with John's message, which was the message Jesus preached during His ministry as well. We'll see that as we go further into studying Mark. Mark is short, so I'll make sure to bring the other Gospels in to further explain what is going on. Does any of that make sense?"

Annie pursed her lips. "So, basically, baptism is just saying you're a die-hard Christian, and you can only be saved by faith. But John's was different, because his baptism said the kingdom of God was coming, because Jesus was there?"

Philippa's smile grew. "Pretty much. Did you know you are one smart cookie?"

Annie looked away, but Philippa didn't miss the smile that was hiding on her face. "Okay, so then why did Jesus have to go out into the wilderness for a month to go be tempted? Why would He want to be tempted?"

Goodness, she asks big questions. But I wouldn't have it any other way. This means she is really trying to understand. "So, Jesus was born man, completely man, and cut Himself off from His Godly power while still remaining fully God. I'm not sure how He cut himself off, but God is God and has no limits, so I trust in His ability to do that. By going to be tempted in the wilderness, he displays that He truly dealt with temptation in His humanity. It is something incredible, in that He could obey the fullness of the Law as a true human. And because He withstood temptation, He can suffer as our true substitute who is completely innocent."

"But why would he want to suffer in our place?" Frustration lined her voice. "Withstanding the challenge of temptation for forty day and then winning only to be headed to a much worse fate seems idiotic."

"Because He loves you and knows that only through his suffering could you ever re-establish relationship with God. He loves you."

"But maybe He shouldn't," Annie snapped. Philippa froze, but Annie continued. "What have I done to deserve love through suffering? My own parents avoid me like the plague. Any chance they have to fight, they take it. They don't love me enough to push past the temptation." Her voice, which had been growing louder, quieted as she whispered, "Maybe they know something that Jesus didn't."

Philippa looked at the girl as her heart broke. *How many times have I thought that? Compared God's love to others. Put my worth in their hands. Doubted God's ability to love me?* Philippa put her hand out and lightly touched the girl's arm. "There is a difference between God and man."

"Yeah, God's all powerful and stuff."

"Yes, but God could have simply destroyed all of the earth once Adam and Eve messed up. A million times God could have simply started over. But He hasn't." Annie didn't say anything, so Philippa continued. "He is powerful, but He also is loving, righteous, and perfect. Your parents are not perfect. I'm sure they do their best, but they live in a broken world and are broken. That's why we pray for them. You and I cannot change their views or if they fight, but we can pray."

"Prayer is just talking to air."

"No. Prayer is a gift to be able to talk to God. A gift paid for in blood." Philippa stared down into the warm drink that was in her hands. "I was a kid when my parents split. I was angry all the time. I would make peace with my life and then another curveball would hit, and I'd be back to my anger. It was this never-ending cycle. I blamed myself for anything and everything. Even more than myself, I blamed God. I told you before about a friend I had in high school that invited me to church. The truth is, I went to make fun of the place. It wasn't until my fourth time coming that I realized that there was something good about the place. Something new to me in the Bible. Hope."

"Yes, but it was misplaced hope. You said it yourself, your parents never got back together."

"But I pray for them. And they may not be back together, but I love them now, and I'm not sure I could say I did back then. I don't have this pent-up anger and aggression towards them. I don't blame myself for what was out of my control. I have peace. It's this peace that I want to share with you, Annie."

Annie looked over toward Charlie and watched him play with the toy cars for several moments before finally saying, "Peace. You found it there?" She nodded over to Philippa's Bible.

"Yes. And you can have it too."

"Teach me."

Chapter Fifteen

Philippa sighed down at the pot of milk that was beginning to look more like cottage cheese than a rue. *I should have known better than to think I could do this on my own.* It was Friday, the end of her first month of watching the kids. Philippa had been so excited about the milestone that she had decided to let the kids choose what they wanted for dinner, but her doom had crashed upon her the second they had said macaroni and cheese. Philippa considered herself proficient in the kitchen but never had she ever been able to make macaroni and cheese. The cheese sauce completely eluded her abilities.

"Philippa? Why do you look like you just watched one of those endangered animal documentaries?" Teressa's voice fizzled from Philippa's phone.

Philippa, never having been good at making mac and cheese, had called the one person she knew could make it perfectly - Teressa. But it seemed that even video chat wouldn't be able to save her.

"I don't think the milk is supposed to be chunky," Philippa groaned.

"Chunky?! Show me!" Philippa did as she was asked and turned her phone camera to the pot. "Oh, no. I think you burned the milk. How did you even do that? The heat is on low, and you only poured the milk in a minute or two ago."

Philippa looked at the burner dial and felt her heart freeze. "Oops!"

"What did you do?"

"I accidently put the burner on high rather than low."

Teressa's baffled expression was hidden by her slap on the forehead. "How can you accidentally do that?!"

Philippa put her phone on the counter beside her and turned the heat off. "I don't know, I guess I just stressed myself out!"

Annie, who was sitting at the counter enjoying the bizarre show of Philippa bumbling around the kitchen laughed. "Pip, it's okay if you can't make mac and cheese."

Before Philippa could assure the girl that she would **not** give up, Teressa squawked on the phone. "Pip?! That's my nickname for you! You're one month into the job, and you have already replaced me!"

Philippa shook her head and rolled her eyes. "You're being silly. Now are you going to help me fix this mess or not? Because if you're not, then I am just going to hang up so you will stop distracting me."

"Fine, fine, fine. Use a ladle and try to get all of the burnt stuff out; we're going to try and salvage as much as we can."

Philippa did what she was told as well as pull the small trash can as close as she could so she could throw away the burnt milk faster. Immersed in her work and her sister's constant yipping with Annie, Philippa didn't hear someone enter the kitchen until Teressa said, "Wow, I haven't met you yet."

Philippa dropped her ladle and turned around. Standing in the kitchen entrance was a tall man. *Oh no. He's come to rob the place! And he's not wearing a mask, so that means he's going to kill Annie and me for seeing his face.* Philippa grabbed the nearest object that wasn't her pot full of lumpy milk. The frying pan was a cold weight in her hand, but she didn't pay it any mind as she looked at the stranger. "Who are you?" She ran to the other side of the counter, so she was in front of Annie.

"I will call the police if you don't leave!" Teressa shouted from her space in the phone. "And I mean it! I have GPS tracking on this phone, so I know exactly where you guys are!"

"You're tracking my phone?!" Philippa yelped.

The man's eyes widened, and he held up his hands, "Whoa, I'm Angela's brother. No need to call the cops or hit me with a pan!" He leaned over to look at Annie who looked just as confused as Philippa felt. "Annie, please tell these lovely ladies who I am."

"Uncle Henry?" Annie asked, squinting at him.

"Do I need to call the police?" Teressa called over to them.

"No," Annie began to chuckle. "This is my Uncle Henry. I didn't recognize him because the last time I saw him, he had a beard bigger than Charlie."

Philippa took a deep breath. It had only been a minute since everything had started happening, but to Philippa it felt like everything had been going so much slower. She turned to look at the stranger and assumed her teacher's position, hands folded in front of her stomach and her smile inviting. The only thing that ruined her serene appearance was the frying pan that was still clutched in her hands. Now that she wasn't afraid Annie was going to get attacked, Philippa could better study the man.

He was at least six feet, with chestnut hair that led to his five o'clock shadow. His pale checkerboard flannel and worn jeans gave him a comfy casual look—definitely not a robber. *I can't believe I was so silly. I need to stop listening to those true crime podcasts if these are the first thoughts that come to mind when people visit.* "My apologies for my brash behavior. My name is Philippa Carol. I'm the kids' new babysitter."

"After a month of watching them, I don't think anyone considers you new!" Teressa shouted over.

Philippa winced. "Pardon me for one moment." It was less than a second for her to hang up on Teressa, but Philippa took pleasure in leaving her sister on the hook. *I can't believe she's been tracking me!* "As I was saying, I'm Philippa Carol," She held out her hand, discreetly putting the frying pan behind her on the counter. "And you are?"

The man thankfully took her outstretched hand and shook it, his calloused hand engulfing hers. "Nice to meet you Philippa Carol. My name is Henry Sulivan, but you can just call me Henry."

Philippa smiled, her real smile coming through her teacher's one. "Then you may call me Philippa."

"I apologize for having startled you. I had assumed Angela would have told you that I was coming today."

"I don't believe she mentioned anything." Philippa turned to look at Annie, her question obvious in her eyes.

Annie shook her head. "Mom didn't say anything about you coming to visit."

Henry gave a rueful smile and shook his head. "She must have been busy and forgotten. I'm very sorry for giving you a fright."

"No, I'm sorry for almost coming at you with a pan." Philippa smiled, but a blush of shame heated her cheeks as she adjusted her glasses. Philippa searched for a topic change when Charlie burst into the room and launched himself onto his uncle. Henry staggered for a mere moment before correcting himself.

"Charlie! How are you little buddy? You being good for your parents?"

Charlie nodded, giggling as he hooked his arms around Henry's leg and sat on his foot.

"Uncle Henry, you came early this year! You'll be here for my birthday!"

Henry shuffled his hand on Charlie's head, messing up his already messy hair. "I sure will, buddy."

Is Charlie's birthday coming up? It's not marked on the calendar. I knew his birthday was in the summer since we celebrated his back in April with all the other summer birthdays, but I didn't know it was coming up so soon. This summer is just flying by. I'll have to ask

Mrs. Johnson what day it is so I can make him a cake or something. I cannot believe I almost missed his birthday! Philippa shook away her thoughts. *I can think about this later, right now I need to focus on what to do next.*

"I am sure you guys have a lot of catching up to do, so I will get back to making dinner, and you all can chat." Philippa turned to the stove, believing that would be all, but then Henry called to her. Turning around, Philippa made sure her teacher's smile didn't show her annoyance. *He has a plot to make sure I mess up this recipe to the point of no return!* "Yes?"

"Would you like any help?"

Before Philippa could say no, Annie answered her, "She desperately needs help. She's making macaroni and cheese, and the cheese sauce isn't going according to plan."

Philippa shot Annie a warning glance. "I will be fine. I just might have to change plans for dinner tonight."

"May I see it?" Henry asked, a polite smile on his face.

His first impressions of me are going to be that I'm a violent menace that can't cook. This is not how I hoped this day would go. Philippa held back a sigh and nodded. They went to the stove, and he stirred the blob that was supposed to be her rue. Philippa could feel her face heat in embarrassment.

"I can fix this," Henry said, turning to face Philippa.

Thank goodness. I didn't mess up as badly as I thought. "You can?" Philippa failed to hide the relief in her voice.

"If you want me to..."

I should just ask him for instructions... but Teressa was giving me instructions, and I still messed it up. "If you wouldn't mind. I'm afraid macaroni and cheese is not in my skillset."

"Yeah, it is a little complex. Let me just get my apron, and I will start."

"May I watch so I can see how I may do better next time?"

"Of course." His face fell into a pleasant smile as he picked up Charlie and threw him onto the counter. "Charlie is my sous-chef, so he can probably tell you all sorts of tips while we work."

"Yeah! Uncle Henry and I have made lots of food. We made waffles last time!"

Philippa laughed and sat at the counter beside Annie to watch. She thought he would go to the entryway where his luggage probably was, but instead he went into the pantry. Out of curiosity, Phillipa glanced in to find him opening a box of oats. Rather than oats, out came a folded piece of black fabric. Henry caught her glance and laughed.

"Horrace and Angela have had the same box of oats since Charlie was born, so I took the oats home a few visits ago and put my apron in for safe keeping."

Philippa nodded, as though this were obvious. "I see." *Thank goodness I haven't tried to make oatmeal cookies yet.*

Henry got right to work, reheating the blob of milk, and pulling out the burnt pieces. Philippa watched in amazement as the monstrosity of a rue turned into something that looked like it could eventually be edible. Henry chatted with the kids as he continued to stir the rue, adding cheese, turning it into a cheese sauce. In the other pot with the already boiled noodles, he added the sauce and let Charlie stir the mixture.

"I don't suppose we have any fresh parsley?" Henry asked.

"Yes, we do actually." Philippa pointed to the fridge.

"We have parsley flakes in the pantry," Annie said.

"That's good to know, but I think fresh would work better for this."

"Fresh is always best." Philippa adjusted her glasses.

"Why?" Annie asked.

"Easy, let me show you." Henry went into the pantry and came out with the jar of parsley flakes and held it, and the bag of fresh parsley up to Annie. "Smell both and tell me which one smells better."

Annie did so. "The fresh smells a little stronger."

"Exactly! It also tastes stronger and better! And it's pretty decoration. Could you get me four plates?" Henry asked.

Annie did as she was told, laying them in a neat line for Henry to add a generous serving upon each one. Philippa picked up two of the plates, the porcelain warm on her fingers.

"Annie, please help me bring the plates into the dining room?"

Annie nodded and the two took the plates into the dining room. The heavy steam coming from the plates made Philippa pause as she sat down.

"The mac and cheese is probably too hot to eat now." *What should we do as we wait?* Philippa looked from Charlie to Annie who were sitting on either side of Henry. "Do you kids want to learn how to make napkin bunnies?"

"Napkin bunnies?" Annie asked as Charlie shouted his approval.

Philippa smiled, "Here, I'll make an example, and then we'll slowly walk through it together."

The kids watched in amazement as she folded the napkin, the soft papery texture gliding through her hands until it stood with two large ears. She set her example in front of all of them and distributed napkins to the kids. Surprisingly, Henry asked for one as well. Philippa kept her teacher's smile in place, hoping her confusion over him wouldn't show in her eyes. As she slowly folded the napkin and explained the instructions, peace filled her.

I've missed teaching. I thought that I was in a new groove, but I do miss my little classroom. Maybe I should bring Mr. Waffles the stuffed animal sometime. Charlie and Annie's first bunnies were a little dopey looking, but Phillipa clapped in joy.

"They're beautiful!"

"Wow, I had no idea that animals were allowed at the table," Henry laughed, placing his wrinkled and deflated napkin on the table beside the others. It looked close to falling at any moment, and the ears were the only thing that looked like they could withstand gravity.

Philippa tried unsuccessfully to hide her amusement over the napkin, but a small tinkling laugh escaped from her. Shame filled her. *I shouldn't laugh at him.* But Henry didn't seem to mind. He laughed and lightly tapped his bunny, making the whole thing topple with a soft humph of air.

"I guess I'll stick to making mac and cheese, and you guys can make sure no more napkins suffer under my lack of skills," he chuckled to himself. "Dinner has probably cooled down by now, let me just pray for the meal, and then we can eat."

He prays! Lord, please let him be a Christian. The kids need more witnesses than just me to teach them about Your glory.

"But it's Annie's turn!" Charlie pouted.

"Annie's turn for what?" Henry asked, his voice pleasant and expression open.

"I have each of us take turns praying for the meals."

Henry gave Philippa a dazzling smile that took her by surprise and bubbled into joy. His smile thus far had been kind and only just reached his eyes, but this smile was different. It was just so warm. His eyes completely crinkled, and it somehow felt full hearted.

"That is a brilliant idea. It truly is genius."

Philippa blushed under the praise. *It really isn't.* "I, um, thank you."

"You can have a turn tonight and then I'll have my turn tomorrow," Annie interjected.

Henry shook his head, still smiling. "No, but thank you. Today is your turn and I would love to hear you pray."

"I'm not very good at it," Annie said bluntly.

"Any prayer from you is more than likely beautiful."

Annie shrugged, but Philippa had to push down her laughter at the sight of the girl's red cheeks. "Fine, you don't have to try and flatter me into praying. Let's bow our heads and close our eyes."

Annie waited for everyone to do as she had asked. "Dear Heavenly Father, I pray that this food would bless us. Thank you for this food and this day. Oh, and for Uncle Henry getting here safely. In Jesus' name, Amen."

"That was beautiful Annie," Henry lightly shook her shoulder, making her giggle.

"It's nowhere near as fancy as the prayers at church," Annie sighed once her laughter had faded.

"The beauty is in the simplicity. I know this guy who has the most elegant wording for his prayers, and they are always super long, but at the end I have no clue what he said. Yours is straight to the point and easy to understand."

"I guess," Annie bit the side of her lip, and Philippa could tell that she didn't believe a word of what he had said.

"Can we eat now?" Charlie whined.

"Yes, squirt," Henry lightly elbowed the small boy.

Dinner was eaten with much laughter and discussion. Philippa only ate a little because she was so immersed in the conversation and the joy of the moment.

Annie's been doing so much better since our Bible study last week. I just wish that she would smile more. I want her to be happy more often, but there's only so much I can do. But getting ready for soccer has made her a lot more excited. Still, Annie is quiet all the time. I suppose all I can do is lift her up to God. He can do so much more than I can, though it's hard to let go and trust Him with someone I care so much about.

But during dinner, Annie was laughing, and if the conversation seemed to come to an end, she would either find a new topic or keep it going. It was so completely foreign, but it made Philippa's spirits soar.

Charlie, lonely Charlie, was having the time of his life having a sword fight using forks with Henry. Henry lost enough times to keep the excitement and pride high but won enough to keep Charlie humble. *I'm so happy that he has a male role model in his life. I know that he and I have a deep relationship, but I don't think he could ever ask his former teacher to have a fork sword fight. Thank You, God, for this man coming here. Thank You for delivering help for the family.*

This moment is beautiful and yet so foreign. My childhood was filled with silent dinners at Mom's as we followed all the dictates of good manners she had drilled into Teressa and me. Dad's house was all about looking through all the cabinets to find dinner, and dinner was whenever people were hungry. We'd never eaten at the table, but instead sat in the living room to see what was on TV. The memories are special, but this loud and joyful table is something I've only ever experienced at pot-blessing at church. The moment was so joyful that butterflies were dancing inside Philippa's stomach.

Faster than she wished, dinner was finished and cleaned up. Philippa placed Dutch Blitz on the table and waited for everyone to get situated. As she had expected, Henry was a speed demon at the game and had wiped them all out in a mere two minutes of starting the game. Even after four more rounds he was still winning and quick. Philippa and the kids had begun counting second place as winners; he was that good.

Philippa's heart fell with the sound of the front door crashing open and shut, a sound she had learned to associate with Mr. Johnson having a bad day at work. She didn't want their fun to be over.

Henry raised an eyebrow at the loud sound, but Philippa minutely shook her head. She made a point of smiling and laughing, trying to distract the kids from looking at the door.

"Alright, I have to go, but you guys should keep playing." The kids turned to look at her, so she decided to further elaborate. "Someone needs to beat your uncle, and I know you two are so close."

Charlie nodded eagerly, "I am so close. I only lost by two last time!"

"I guess we could keep playing," Annie said, not as easily distracted as her brother.

"Yeah, guys. Let's keep playing, that is, if you're not too scared," Henry baited.

"We're not scared," Annie rose in her chair. "We can beat you. We just keep letting you win so your tiny ego doesn't shatter like your dignity."

"Ooh, Annie. You've been saving that up, huh?" Henry chuckled.

Philippa itched to correct the girl and tell her to be more kind but knew that this was all just silly banter. *I need to get going. If I don't leave soon, I won't have enough time to prepare the meat for Sunday's barbeque.* Her mind made up, she gave each child a side hug and waved goodbye to Henry.

She felt a twinge of sadness to leave all the fun, but her sense of duty was stronger than her desire to be part of their moment. *It's for the best. They need time to hang out and catch up with their uncle without my interference.* So she drove home, humming along to the radio as her heart still danced to the beat of the laughter that she had left.

Chapter Sixteen

Saturday flew past, and before Philippa knew it, she was opening the doors of the church. The scent of pastries and coffee were a familiar scent, however there were more savory scents to the mix this morning. As Philippa walked through the entrance, she basked in the sun streaming through the windows that warmed her skin and made the tables against the far-left wall glow.

Once a month, the church held what was called a pot-blessing. Every person brought a meal to contribute, and then everyone got to fill their plates with the different meals and enjoy being together. It was Philippa's favorite time of the month, even though her arms burned from balancing two pots and her Bible bag in her arms.

Charice, in a more muted maroon dress that made her skin appear even warmer than usual, approached her. Unsurprisingly, she was sipping a large cup of coffee as she took her place beside Philippa and gave her a half hug.

"Girl, what'd you bring today? It smells spicy," Charice asked, lowering her paper coffee cup from her lips. She gave Philippa a dazzling smile as she breathed in deeply.

"It's spicy Mongolian beef. I also brought rice to place the meat onto. The juices and seasoning seep into the rice and you get to enjoy the flavors from the meat with the joy that is rice."

Rice was a funny thing for Philippa. When she was a child, she hated it. But now, it reminded her of her family and gave her a small burst of warmth. However, she still didn't like the taste of it, so putting other, more flavorful, foods on top was how she got through it.

"Oh, that sounds good. I brought my grandma's chili, but I think it might be a tad too spicy for everyone else here."

Philippa giggled, placing her large pot of meat and smaller pot of rice down on the table with all of the other food. Charice had always lived in Maine, but that didn't change that she felt that no one in the small New England state had strong enough taste buds.

Charice strode over to a large red Dutch oven pot that Philippa recognized from Charice's house. She opened the pot and took a big whiff of the steam that came out. Three feet away, Philippa almost coughed at the severe amount of spice that had come from just the steam.

"Oh, Charice. That might be more than a tad too much spice."

"It just smells too spicy. Trust me, it tastes a lot more bland. Well, usually it does, I kind of went off the recipe when I was seasoning it."

Philippa playfully groaned. "How much chili powder did you add?"

Charice tilted her head and pursed her lips. "Not, sure. It's kind of hard to tell. I had a whole bottle of it when I started, and now it's almost three-fourths empty. So more than a little."

Philippa shook her head but laughed. "You need to learn some self-control."

"I do have self-control; I just don't have seasoning control. Come with me while I get another cup of coffee, and then we can wait at my desk until church starts."

Philippa did as Charice suggested, getting herself a cup of lavender chamomile tea as Charice added all the extra flavors into her coffee. The two girls talked at the front desk for several minutes, catching up and talking about random useless topics that made them both laugh.

"Come on, you can't really like Mr. Darcy more than Bath Man," Charice whined, keeping her coffee close so she could sip it after every sentence. Bathman was a famous superhero comic strip that had grown into movies and television shows.

"I suppose Bathman in 1966 was a hero, but the Bathman in the recent movies is all about vengeance rather than justice."

"He's heroic and has enough muscles to open a pickle jar without struggling for fifteen minutes."

"I suppose, but how heroic is it if he is always killing people and putting more lives in danger? The Jester's antics got more dangerous once he had what he considered a rival."

"Aw, that's not Bruce's fault."

"No, it's not, but if we followed the story through a civilian's eyes, wouldn't both of them be seen as the villain? Through that lens, there isn't much to defend his honor."

"Ugh, can't you just appreciate the finer things in life? Like looking at him."

"Charice!" Philippa lightly slapped her friend's arm, the sound of a muffled tap.

"What? Someone had to say it."

Philippa shook her head, blinking when Charice put down her coffee and gave a brilliant smile, looking over Philippa's shoulder.

"Greetings, I'm Charice."

"Hello." Philippa turned around at the sound of the decidedly male voice.

Henry stood three feet away from her, looking directly at her. Today he wore a deep green button up with blue trousers. Philippa was frozen in surprise, unsure of what to do. *He's here? I had assumed that he was religious, but why is he here? Where're the Johnsons? Surely, he came with them.*

"Welcome. We're happy to have you visiting this morning."

Philippa could have bought her friend four coffees right then and there. *Thank you for saving me from my own awkwardness!* Philippa snapped out of her surprise and went immediately into teacher greeting mode. Her hands folded in front of her waist, and she gave a small sincere smile.

Henry turned to Charice who was standing behind her desk. "It's good to be here. My name is Henry. You may know my sister, Angela Johnson."

Charice blinked in surprise but didn't miss a beat. "You're Angela's brother?"

"Yes, I am. So, you know her?"

"Not very well, but Philippa here," Charice gestured to Philippa, "works for her. She has been watching the kids while your sister and brother-in-law work."

Henry turned to Philippa and gave her a quick smile. "Yes, we met on Friday." He gave Philippa his full attention. Philippa hadn't realized it earlier, but he was carrying a brown Bible bag as well as a small multi-plant potting set in his right hand. Even more surprising was when he used his left hand to grab the planter and offered it to her. "I brought this for you to say sorry for scaring you on Friday."

Philippa blushed and wanted to sink her head into her shoulders. *No! I refuse to do anything as undignified as that!* "Oh, that really isn't necessary. I should be bringing you a peace offering after I almost hit you with that pan."

"You tried to hit him with a pan?" Charice gasped.

Philippa's blush deepened. "I had assumed he was robber."

"In her defense," Henry laughed, "I did just show up. I thought Angela would have told her I was coming, otherwise I would have knocked rather than just making my way in."

Philippa wanted the ground to swallow her up whole. She was completely ashamed of her actions on Friday and could feel her face bursting in flames, but Henry didn't seem at all fazed by the conversation. If anything, he looked pleased. *Lord, please have mercy on me and give me a good excuse to run away.*

Philippa cleared her throat and pulled her hair behind her ear, hoping she hadn't ruined the flower she had clipped behind her ear. "Yes, well, um, I shouldn't have started with violence."

Charice, who was vibrating in excitement, blurted out, "Philippa, I always knew there was a shred of violence in you."

"Charice," Philippa hissed.

"What? Let me have this moment. I always assumed you were like some sort of angel that had come down to show off your grace and peace, but now I can rest in peace knowing that my chaotic ways have rubbed off on you."

Philippa smiled at Henry. "I'm sorry, my friend has been deeply troubled for many years."

"And now you have a twisted sense of humor too!" Charice beamed. "I am so proud of you. Hold on, let me find my phone to take a picture to commemorate the moment."

Philippa shook her head, turning her full attention to Henry. "Welcome to our church. Normally we aren't this barbaric."

Henry chuckled, the deep sound making the hairs at the back of Philippa's neck stand. "There is nothing barbaric about two friends teasing each other. But here, let me do what I came here to do." He again held the planter up in offering. "This has Rosemary, Cilantro, Basil, and Parsley. I wrote a little care instruction card that you can use. Since you were talking about how fresh is better while we were making mac and cheese, I thought that you might appreciate having fresh herbs in your kitchen."

Philippa's shoulders lowered as she smiled down at the gift. *No one's ever known about my love of plants.* Since she was a small girl,

Philippa had always wanted to have her own garden, but with no clue of how to start one, she had always pushed it off, saying maybe tomorrow. "Thank you," Philippa took the planter in her hand, touched by the thoughtfulness. "But you really didn't have to. You did nothing to apologize for."

Henry's smile softened. "Then consider it a thank you. The last time I visited my sister, the kids weren't in good shape. How did you know to put Annie into soccer? I haven't seen her this excited since she was five, and I had bought her a doll."

Philippa, thankful for the conversation change that wouldn't make her cheeks burst into flames, forced herself to look away from the gift. "Ah, that actually was quite simple. I take them to the park almost daily, and she always goes for the soccer ball. During a divorce, it's easy to feel alone, so I wanted to get her into a program where she was around people doing something she loves. Charice is actually a co-coach as well, so I know that the program isn't going to end in a dumpster fire."

"Aw, that's the nicest thing you have ever said about me."

Henry chuckled at Charice but continued. "It may have been simple for you, but that doesn't change that it meant the world to her. You have my thanks."

Philippa's cheeks warmed. *So much for being done blushing.* "You have nothing to thank me for."

"No—"

"Philippa, dear," Mrs. White called from the entryway. "Church is going to begin in two minutes."

Philippa jumped and looked at the clock. *How did I lose track of time?*

"Sorry, Mrs. White. I'm coming." Philippa turned to Henry. "I apologize, but I have to go play the entry music. It was a pleasure to see you. Will you stay for the pot-blessing?" Henry looked over to the far table that was covered in double the food than when Philippa had first arrived. "Of course."

Philippa gave a small smile and speed walked into the sanctuary, heading to the piano. Carla, the main pianist, occasionally had Philippa play the intro so she could get her newborn baby situated in the children's room. Philippa approached the piano and fit her fingers onto the smooth keys. *Thank you for this day, God. May You be glorified by my playing, and may I have a heart of worship as I play. Amen.*

Chapter Seventeen

The moment Pastor Tom had ended and invited everyone to fellowship during the pot-blessing, the congregation erupted into conversation as they made their way out of the sanctuary. The people streamed into the entry room which had been filled with tables and chairs, ready for everyone to sit and eat together.

The line for food was long and loud as people continued their conversations. Philippa, content with everyone else getting their food first, went back into the sanctuary to reflect on the sermon before she got lost in the fun. The sermon had been centered on Philippians 1:27-31.

Philippa sat in the center back of the church and stared past the wooden pews to the large cross that hung on the center wall directly across from her. Verse twenty-nine kept playing through her mind as she immersed herself in the view.

For it has been granted to you
that for the sake of Christ
You should not only believe in him,

but also suffer for his sake.

Philippa was reminded of the bad times in her life. Getting rejected by her dream school, her family getting divorced, losing her house. The sadness and the fear of the moments were still strong, like an old friend that never quite left. *Through all those moments, was my manner worthy of the gospel of Christ? Did I stand firm? Was I a good witness?* She couldn't say for sure.

Dear Heavenly Father, You are greater than I can imagine; You rule with justice and righteousness. Your thoughts are higher than mine. Your plans are higher than mine. Teach me to rest in Your glory. Give me the strength to stand firm in Your word. May my actions and words reflect You and point those around me to You. May this all be for Your glory. In Jesus' name, Amen.

With her prayer concluded, she turned to get up and leave, only to find Henry standing at the doorway. He gave her a quick smile and came to the pew in front of hers and sat as well.

"That was a good sermon," he commented, turning so that he sat sideways, looking at her while still able to see the front of the church.

"Indeed, it was. I'm glad you liked it." Philippa pushed down her awkwardness and kept her expression open and joyful.

"I appreciated how Pastor – I'm sorry, what was his name again?"

"Tom." Philippa, her hands out of view, twisted the small red pen she kept in her skirt pocket.

"That's what it was. I appreciated how Pastor Tom consistently went back to the Bible to support his sermon. And he gave context!

I have visited a lot of different churches, and I have concluded that context can make or break an argument."

Philippa nodded. "It's very important to understand the context of any passage you read. It's intriguing how erratically a verse can change based on context."

"Indeed. So, what did you think of this morning's sermon."

"Well, like many, I love the book of Philippians. I've studied it numerous times, and yet every time I come to it, I find something new that I didn't notice or fully comprehend before. Today, the verse about suffering for Christ stuck out, especially remembering that is the theme that carries through chapter two as well."

"There is a lot of suffering. It's humbling to remember that we are promised to suffer for Him. There was a friend I had who was in the missions field, and when I asked him how he could deal with all the pain of constantly being in danger and under attack, he merely replied with 'What bliss to suffer for Christ's name.'" He paused and looked over to the cross.

"That is beautiful," Philippa smiled softly at the cross. The discussion of suffering reminded Philippa of Annie and Charlie. They were suffering, and she wasn't sure if they had the hope of Christ to comfort them. "I wish things were different for the kids."

She had made the comment without thinking, but Henry turned and gave her his full attention. "The kids? Are you talking about Annie and Charlie?"

Philippa nodded. "I just want them to have some peace during the tragedy that is raining down around them?"

"Tragedy? Are you talking about the divorce?"

Philippa blinked. "Of course. It's awful to see a family torn apart."

"But it's what's best for everyone."

Philippa pulled back and fixed her expression into her teacher's expression. "I'm sorry. I spoke without thinking."

"Divorce isn't great, but Angela and Horrace have been fighting for years. They can't keep on going like this."

There was a pause of silence until Philippa finally replied, softly, "I know it's hard." *Lord, please give me the words.* "Seeing loved ones hurting always is. But if you feel this way, may I encourage you to read Matthew 19?"

Henry sighed and looked back at the cross. "I have read it often, but I still don't understand why divorce is so wrong when two people can't work it out."

Philippa took a deep breath as she thought through what to do. "Maybe read Matthew 19 while remembering what it says in Malachi 2." Philippa opened her Bible and flipped over to Malachi. "Verse 16 says 'For I hate divorce,' says Yahweh, the God of Israel." Philippa looked up from her worn Bible pages into Henry's eyes. "If the God of love hates divorce, doesn't that give us a hint as to how wrong it is?"

Henry rubbed his jaw. "That is very straight forward."

"There is only one example in the Bible where divorce is okay, and that's when a spouse has been unfaithful. There isn't much I know about the Johnsons, but I do know that they are faithful." Philippa sighed. "It's not my place to try and push you into one opinion or the other. I think you should talk with Pastor Tom, and the two of you can work through the problems together by centering the solution in the scriptures."

"I believe I will talk to Pastor Tom. Thank you for your insight. For now, why don't we go join the others for the pot-blessing?"

Philippa smiled and rose from her seat. "That sounds perfect."

Henry reached the end of his pew first but waited for her and gestured for her to go first. Stepping into the entry room, Philippa was glad to see that the line was significantly shorter, but there were still three or four people, so they wouldn't be completely out of place getting their food so much later than everyone else. Philippa led Henry over to the serving table where she got a large plate and filled it with tiny servings of everything the table had to offer. Henry's plate was filling fast due to the large serving size that he got of the meals. He stopped in front of Charice's large red pot and took a sniff at the chili. He coughed three times and blinked in surprise.

"Sorry, Charice doesn't know how to control herself when it comes to seasonings," Philippa giggled.

"Charice made this?" He paused at her nod, looking from her to the chili, before finally getting a large scoop onto his plate.

Philippa's eyebrows rose in surprise, but she kept her silence. *Maybe he's psychotic?* With her plate full, and a small cup of tea in her hands, she navigated her way to the center table where Charice and Mrs. White were sitting. Unused to the sight of two empty spots at the table, it took Philippa a moment to realize that one must be meant for Henry.

Charice must want to make him feel more welcome. Philippa took a seat and a few seconds later Henry joined them, sitting to her right.

"Henry! You have a rather large portion of my chili," Charice said, leaning around Philippa to better see him.

Henry smiled and laughed. "Yes, it smelled like it was wonderfully seasoned, so I thought it would be worth a try."

Charice chuckled, an evil smirk tilting her lips. "Most are too scared to. You'd think they would remember that one verse in today's sermon. The one about not being frightened about anything. Pastor Tom needs to use my food in one of his sermons and tell everyone that if they are scared by something as miniscule as my cooking, then they aren't going to fare very well in the real world."

Philippa shook her head. "You're misquoting it, and it's not that any of us are afraid of your cooking. We just have better survival instincts." Philippa paused, realizing that her words might be taken offensively by Henry. She quickly turned and was relieved to find him laughing. *He's very well-mannered and lighthearted,* she absentmindedly thought.

Henry took a tentative bite of the chili. He lasted two seconds, which was two seconds longer than anyone at the table had thought he would last, before he began a coughing fit and gulped down his entire cup of water.

His face was still red, and his nose was running as he said, "You're right, everyone else has better survival instincts."

Surprised by the humor, Philippa began laughing. It was a small giggle that grew into something that seemed to echo in her. Leaning back so she could lean on her also-dying-of-laughter friend, Philippa found peace in the moment as she and Henry's eyes locked, and they both smiled with red faces.

Chapter Eighteen

Monday morning, Philippa lightly sipped her tea as she waited for Mrs. Johnson to talk with her in the entryway before leaving for work. The memory of Mrs. Johnson rushing by, telling her that she wanted to have a small chat played through her mind as Philippa breathed in the steam of her blueberry tea.

This morning had been surprisingly brisk and foggy. *I wonder if the park is going to be soaked from the night's mist. I'm not opposed to taking the kids to the park and having fun in the wet grass, but I highly doubt that the other kids will be there. Perhaps we will try a different venue for the day?*

"Ms. Carol."

Philippa turned and gave her teacher's smile to Mrs. Johnson. "Good morning, Ma'am."

"Good morning. I apologize for what happened on Friday. Henry told me everything," Mrs. Johnson lightly pulled the bottom of her pale pink shirt, making it more taut.

Shame filled Philippa at the memory of almost attacking Henry. After spending so much time with him the day before, she had come to learn that he was a really kind person, which made her feel even more guilty for her brash reaction. "There is nothing to apologize for. I reacted badly when I should have welcomed your brother.

Mrs. Johnson shook her head briskly. "Nonsense. I had merely forgotten to warn you of his arrival. I am glad to know that if an intruder came here, you would protect my children. Henry will be staying with my family until the trial is over with, but I would still like you to watch the kids."

Philippa paused. It hadn't occurred to her that Henry could just watch the kids on his own. "Yes, ma'am."

"Originally, I was going to have my brother take over, but he has made me aware that he will be working on multiple projects over the summer, and the kids will do very well if you remain a constant in their life."

Philippa nodded. "I am happy to be there for your family."

"And we appreciate that, more than you can know. I'm sorry, but I really must get going."

Mrs. Johnson walked past her and exited the house. Philippa took a deep breath, feeling more than a little off balance after the conversation. The idea that her employment had been hanging so precariously and she had had no idea bothered her. She had been watching the kids for a month, and yet, she didn't know what she would do with herself if it all went away. And it almost had. *I need to prepare myself for the day it does happen, because I can't watch them for the rest of our lives.* That aching pain filled her. The fear of change and loss right at her fingertips and hazing her thoughts. Philippa shook away the feeling, though it lingered. She made her way to the kitchen, hoping to leave the feeling in the entryway.

"Hello."

The sudden voice made Philippa jump. Her eyes focused, and she finally took in her surroundings. Standing behind the counter was Henry. He was already wearing his apron and had a deep brown flannel on. "Sorry, I didn't mean to scare you. Again." He lightly chuckled as he shook his head. "I'm going to start wearing a bell."

Philippa smiled. "Nonsense, then I would think that we were being robbed by a fleet of Christmas elves."

"Yes, that would be a problem. So, what are we making for breakfast?"

"We? Mrs. Johnson told me you have multiple projects to work on this summer. I can work on breakfast."

Henry waved his hand in the air in a shooing motion. "I have the next few days free." He went over to the fridge and opened the doors. "I was thinking we would make biscuits and gravy, but I am flexible."

Philippa blinked twice before joining him at the fridge. "Biscuits and gravy sound like a great idea, but we don't have any sausage or bacon, so it will be a little hard to add the flavor fats to the gravy."

"No worries, I bought sausage last night." Out from behind the eggs, he pulled out a package of eight sausage links. "Horrace loves sausage, so I was hiding them behind something he would be too lazy to touch."

"Eggs?"

"Yep. He likes eggs but hates cleaning the pan after eating them, so he would never touch them. One of my smarter hiding spots since it's in clear sight."

Philippa shook her head. "I'm afraid your hiding spot is flawed. Mr. Johnson has been boiling eggs to make egg salad for his lunches."

Henry's shoulders fell. "I knew it would have been too good to be true."

Philippa's laugh chimed in the room as she shook her head, turning away from the fridge to go look into the pantry. Running her fingertips across the smooth cardboard boxed foods she stopped at the biscuit mix. She pulled it off its shelf and made her way to the produce section of the pantry. She grabbed apples and cinnamon before exiting the small room. She put her findings onto the counter, looking up to find that Henry had already pulled out all the ingredients needed for a basic gravy.

"So did you plan all this last night, or did you wake up and have a craving for biscuits and gravy?"

"Both." He pulled a large glass mixing bowl out from under the counter. "You can make the biscuits while I get started on the sausages."

Philippa nodded and began working immediately. The biscuits were done in moments and ready to enter the oven once it finished preheating. With the extra time she had, she began cutting two apples into slices and adding the small flourishes she had loved as a child. With a small dash of cinnamon, the apples were done and plated with enough time for Philippa to place the biscuits into the first oven.

Henry, just finishing the sausages, whistled lowly. "You make fast work. If you ever think of going into gardening let me know. I would hire you in a second. A third of my men don't have even a smidgen of your productivity."

Philippa blushed at the praise and shrugged. "So that's what your job is? Gardening?"

"Yep. I work on starting and maintaining new growth to help city environments. Usually, I just monitor the health of plants, but occasionally I'm consulted on what to do to completely uproot and restart gardens."

"That's so neat." *That means the instructions for the herbs he gave to me are probably really good. I should be careful to not kill the plants; I would hate to offend him.* "So did you always want to get into the gardening business, or did you land on that after wandering?"

"It's a little more complex than that. I have always loved working outside and the science of how these living things can grow from the ground and help shape entire ecosystems. It has always fascinated me, but since I was a small boy, I've wanted to get into the missions field. I think someday I will, but for now, I'm a gardener."

Carefully, he poured the sausage grease into the small pot he was making the gravy in. He began whisking, and Philippa was given the moment to think about what he had said.

"When I was a kid, I wanted to become a professional scuba diver."

Henry pulled back, paused, and turned to look at her. "A scuba diver?"

Philippa giggled. "Yes, it was the closest thing I could think of at the time which would make me a mermaid."

"I remember when Angela was in her mermaid phase. I don't think she ever considered becoming a scuba diver; you must have been a big fan."

"A little too big." Philippa went around the counter to sit on one of the stools. Putting her elbows on the table, she rested her chin on her hands. "I eventually gave up on the idea when my little sister told me that real mermaids are scaly like snakes."

"Oof, harsh truth."

"Yeah, she was a wicked little kid." Philippa closed her eyes as the memory of little Teressa filled her thoughts. She had always been in the dirt, and her hands were usually sticky, something that had annoyed Philippa as a child, but she missed now. Philippa's eyes fluttered open, and she shook away the nostalgia. "It wasn't until I was in high school that I decided I wanted to be a teacher."

"What made you want to teach?"

Philippa sighed and a bittersweet smile crossed her face before she corrected her expression. "In sophomore year there was this classmate who just could not grasp geometry. I became close with her, and we usually went to the library after school where I would have to completely reteach what we had learned earlier in the day. I guess after a while of tutoring her, I figured out I love teaching."

"That's neat."

"Hi, Ms. Carol and Uncle Henry," Charlie skipped into the room. "What 'cha talking about?"

"Morning, Charlie," Henry made a silly face at the small boy.

"Good morning," Philippa smiled at Charlie. "We were talking about our dream jobs when we were kids. Do you have a dream job?"

Charlie nodded enthusiastically. "I am going to be a cowboy."

Henry raised his hand and the two high fived. "Good choice, little man."

"What are you making for breakfast?"

"Biscuits and gravy. The gravy will take a little longer to cook."

Charlie's shoulders lowered. "But I'm hungry now."

Philippa shook her head at him. "Charlie, mind your manners. Come over here, and you may have a cinnamon apple bunny."

Charlie ran the few steps to come to her side. Philippa gave him two and he sat on the stool beside her. Henry tilted his head at the plate of apple slices.

"I like the way you made the apples. They look like the napkins you guys folded on Friday. Are bunnies your favorite animal?"

"No, but they are my mother's favorite. She taught my sister and I how to find bunnies in everything. It's been a surprisingly useful gift."

"I imagine so."

Annie came down a few minutes later, and soon all of them were eating breakfast together. The food was delicious, and the conversation loud and heart filling. Philippa kept her additions to the conversation to a minimum, but after everyone had washed their plates, Philippa made certain she had the two kids' attention.

"Because Annie has soccer practice at three, I think a change in venue would be a good idea for this morning."

"Where would we go?" Annie's eyebrows furrowed as though it had never occurred to her that there were other places to spend time at.

"The library, of course."

"The library?" Charlie scrunched his tiny nose in disgust. "But the library is boring. We have to be really quiet in there."

Philippa nodded, "You do when you're inside, but I'm going to show you my favorite spot, where you can be as loud as you want, keeping in mind not to use your panic volume." *I'm so grateful I learned to teach my students the different volumes. If I remember correctly, Charlie had a good understanding of the concept of appropriate volume levels.*

"I guess that will be okay," Annie said, biting her lip. "But I was hoping to get in some more practice before 3."

"We can kick the ball around a little while we're there, if you want, but I think you need to get your mind off of soccer for a few hours."

"May I tag along?" Henry asked.

"If you would like." *This is perfect. He will be a good distraction for Annie. I can tell that she's nervous about soccer practice.* "Annie, go and get your soccer things, and we can put them into my trunk."

Annie nodded, and soon everyone got into Philippa's car, ready to find out where one could be loud at the library.

Philippa and the group stood in front of the large brick library. The library was one of the older buildings in the community, but it always felt fresh and new whenever she stood in front of its thick wooden doors. She desperately wanted to go inside and immerse herself in one of the books that awaited her, but she forced herself to turn away from the door.

"Come along, we'll go around the side," Philippa told her group.

"Around the side? Why?" Annie asked, bewilderment written across her narrowed face.

"From the look Ms. Philippa just gave the building, I assume that is so she doesn't get distracted by the books," Henry laughed.

Philippa's cheeks heated in embarrassment. *He's only known me for a few days, and already he can interpret how easily distracted I am when it comes to books.* His knowledge of her gave her a weird feeling. It was the feeling she got right before a rollercoaster went down a big hill, or the moment before her students performed for their parents. *How strange, I must be allergic to something nearby.*

Philippa shook away the odd feeling and continued leading the way to her favorite spot. They made their way past the alleyway that encircled the side of the library building. Turning the corner to arrive at the back of the library building, everyone paused to soak in the view that was completely hidden to the rest of the world.

Lucious green grass, evenly trimmed, swayed lightly in the wind, interrupted only by the stone path that led to the dark wooden gazebo. Floral bushes surrounded the edges of the gazebo, stems twirling around the support beams, their soft scent swirling through the air. An oak tree stood tall behind the gazebo, its leaves and branches providing shade from the beaming sun that had finally been freed from the morning's clouds.

Phillippa turned and looked nervously at the rest of her group, waiting to figure out how they felt about the view. *What are they thinking? Maybe I should have done what I always do with people. Coffee shops exist for a reason.* But coffee didn't feel like this. The fresh air, the warmth of the sun, and the bright colors that sang the Lord's praises in their beauty. This place always felt more alive, and for a reason she couldn't understand, she wanted the kids and Henry to see it. To enjoy the hidden treasure with her.

Charlie was the first to move; he ran over to the large open space and began to run around, jumping and doing cartwheels all over the place. Annie was slower to get comfortable. She cautiously strolled over to the gazebo, looking inside it as if there were some more secrets in the plain architecture. Henry stayed beside Philippa, content with looking at the view. It was some moments before he finally said something, breaking the awkwardness that had been pressing upon Philippa's shoulders.

"It's lovely. How did you ever find it?"

Philippa sighed gratefully, her shoulders lowering in relief. It was odd that his opinion of this spot mattered, but she was happy to see that he also enjoyed the view. "I used to study and grade homework in the library, at a table by the window just over there." she pointed to a window on the second floor. "The problem with working by a window is that I get distracted by what's outside the window. I saw the top of the gazebo and was intrigued, so I asked the librarian if there was any way to the back. She showed me the back door and then told me that you could also walk around the building to get there. I guess I've been in love ever since."

"With a view like this, I can understand why."

His smile was small, resting on his face in an open expression of appreciation as he looked across the green field. Philippa's heart warmed at his enjoyment of the simple place.

"The beauty is in its simplicity," Philippa said, remembering his praise for Annie's prayer.

His gaze finally left the expanse and turned to her, his small smile growing. Charlie cartwheeled in front of Philippa and Henry, breaking the moment. She smiled down at Charlie, mentally pulling herself out of her desire to just sit and stare for the rest of the day, getting lost in thoughts and dreams.

Philippa strolled over to the gazebo, keeping her steps on the rock path. The gazebo had benches of the same wood attached to the walls. Philippa set her backpack down and opened the largest pocket, pulling out what she hoped would be powerful enough to help Annie forget about her nerves until practice.

The others stood in the center of the field, waiting to see what Philippa had in mind. Philippa was a good distance away from them but shrugged the tiniest hairs width. *I really hope Henry won't mind. And I hope he catches it.*

With a speed only great amounts of practice could obtain, Philippa aimed herself and flung the canary yellow frisbee to Henry. His eyes widened in surprise, but he reached out and caught it. A wicked smile that matched the gleam in his eyes spread across his face. He ran further to put distance between himself and the kids. He turned while running and threw it into the air calling out Charlie's name.

Charlie lit up with excitement and tumbled slightly to catch the frisbee that was a foot or two to his left. Charlie, with the wobbliness of an eight-year-old, threw it to Annie. Phillippa watched, holding her breath to see if the girl would join in. Annie looked over to Philippa for less than a second, but Philippa didn't miss the look of competitiveness in her eyes and smirk. Annie ran, jumping to catch the wayward frisbee.

Annie cheered in celebration before swinging it toward Henry, who had to jump to catch it. Henry gave Philippa an evil smile, but she took no mind to it. She and her fellow classmates in college used to play frisbee all the time. There was no way any of them could beat her. Philippa was humble in most of her skills, but frisbee was something she felt she'd earned the ability to brag about. Unfortunately, frisbee throwing wasn't a skill that was very useful as a teacher.

The frisbee throwing went on for a while until all of them were sweaty and tired. They sat in the gazebo and ate the lunch that Philippa had packed. Annie and Philippa were all rested up when it was time for Annie to go to practice. The drive to the soccer fields was short, so Annie was a few minutes early. Henry opted to watch Charlie, and the two of them went across the way to the small playground that was beside the soccer field, leaving Philippa and Annie to watch as the other girls clustered together.

Philippa could feel the nervousness ooze off of Annie. Without thinking, Philippa took Annie's hand and squeezed her fingers.

"You are going to be great. You have a beautiful soul, don't forget that."

Annie didn't look up, her eyes focused onto the other girls. "What if I'm not good enough?"

Philippa lightly grasped Annie's shoulders and turned her to meet her gaze. "Then we try again next year. I know you're afraid, but while this moment is scary, it's only a single moment. Life moves on. In the Bible, the book of Isaiah has a verse that says 'Do not fear, for I am with you; do not be afraid, for I am your God. I will strengthen you; I will surely help you; I will uphold you with My right hand of righteousness.' Remember what we've been studying in Mark? With Jesus calming the storm?"

Annie nodded. "Yes, he told the storm to have peace and be still, then told the disciples that they had little faith since they were afraid."

"I know that you are afraid right now, but you can trust in God. You can rest in his peace. Let me pray with you for a moment, and then you should go and sit with the other girls." Annie nodded, her shoulders lowering in surrender as she closed her eyes and bowed her head. "Dear Heavenly Father, I pray for peace for Annie. I pray that You would lead her and give her the courage she needs. Lord,

I pray that she would get onto the team, but we trust in Your plan even if she doesn't get on the team. In Jesus' name, Amen."

Annie opened her eyes and didn't look any less scared; however, she walked over to the other girls. Philippa took a seat on the grass beside some of the parents that had decided to stay and watch their kids. *Lord, please guide her.*

Halfway through the try outs, Philippa was thrilled and filled with pride as Annie excelled in all the trials. Henry sat beside Philippa, his sudden presence making her jump.

"Where's Charlie?"

Henry smiled and pointed at the playground where Philippa could clearly see Charlie playing with a bunch of other kids. "I needed to sit down. I used to think I had good stamina, but running around with him all day has me second guessing myself. I thought I'd sit with you since your spot gives good visual on both the kids. How's Annie doing?"

Philippa smiled, her pride shining through her usual teacher's smile. "She is doing phenomenally. She was nervous at the beginning, but I think she's figured out her groove. She's even joking around with the other girls."

Henry smiled, easing back slightly, but keeping his eyes on Charlie. "That's good. She's acting a lot more like she used to. A few years ago, she started getting down, and it's only worsened as time has gone by."

"Yes, I was similar at her age."

"You?" Henry raised an eyebrow in surprise.

"My parents got divorced when I was young."

"Oh."

Philippa wanted to laugh; it was the first time she had ever seen him speechless. "I was a loud child, but when their fighting started and didn't end, I became quiet. When they told us, my sister and I, that they were getting a divorce, I drew into myself. I felt all alone, and somehow, I blamed myself for my parents always fighting."

Henry was silent for a moment, thinking about what she had said. "Do you think that's what's happening with Annie? She's blaming herself?"

Philippa could still hear Annie's broken voice. *What did I do wrong?* "Yes. I think that she blames herself, and that she's scared of what is coming. It sounds like, with the split, she will now have two houses, but neither will feel like home. One house may be a nightmare, or both will be bliss, but either way she is going to hear her parents paint each other as the bad guy. It's confusing and heartbreaking."

The two sat in silence, watching both kids run around and have fun in their own respective games. *Why did I tell him all of that?* Philippa didn't like talking about her parents, and she really didn't like to talk about the divorce. She briefly glanced at Henry, taking in his solemn expression. *Oh no. I've depressed the fun uncle!*

"I'm beginning to understand what you said yesterday. I had assumed everyone would be happier once Angela and Horrace split, but I hadn't thought about what comes after. The moving between the houses, the blame, especially the kids blaming themselves." Henry turned his full attention to Philippa, occasionally glancing at Charlie to ensure the child was safe. Philippa found it hard to breathe at the look of sorrow in his eyes. "I just want my sister to be happy."

Philippa's hands twiddled together as she played with her nail, trying desperately to find the words. *Lord, please give me guidance. May my words be glorifying to You.* "I understand that, but is there no other way to find peace?"

Henry pulled on a small blade of grass, folding it and turning it over in his hands. "Once again, you've given me a question that I don't know how to answer."

"I apologize."

"No, no." Henry waved his hand in the air, shooing away the apology. "I suppose I am used to plants. I almost always know how to help a plant that is struggling, so this whole situation is throwing me off because I don't know how to help."

"Just being here is helping. You're a bright spot in the kids' lives. However, speaking of plants, is that what your projects are for the summer? Gardening?"

"Yes, I have a few clients that I help with tending their gardens. I usually come here during the summer to be with Angela and the kids, but I also like this community. If there wasn't so much snow in the winter, I would move here, but it's a little hard to be a gardener when there is snow."

Philippa laughed. "That's New England for you."

"Have you lived here all your life? What drew you to this small corner of the world?"

Philippa pulled the red pen out of her bun, her silky black hair falling in straight locks around her. With the pen in her hand, she twirled the cap on and off, her hands happy to have something to fidget with. "I'm originally from Minnesota but went to college in Arizona. I figured out quickly that, while I liked Arizona, I did not like the heat, so I moved to Maine where I applied to all the elementary schools in the area, and I finally landed at Charlie's school. I suppose the job is what drew me here, but my church is what has kept me here."

"Yes, your church is a charming motley crew."

"Uncle Henry!" Charlie called over. Philippa looked over to see him swinging on the monkey bars. "Look! I'm doing it!"

"Good job, buddy!" Henry turned to look at Philippa. "I should get back to him."

Philippa bowed her head and smiled. "Have fun!"

Henry chuckled. "I'll try."

Chapter Nineteen

"I'm not sure I understand. Is Friday a holiday?" Philippa asked, truly bewildered.

Mrs. Johnson shook her head then paused. "Not a national holiday. It's Charlie's birthday, and Horrace and I have both taken the day off to celebrate together as a family, as this will be the last birthday we celebrate together."

Philippa nodded, her concern easing and being replaced by bubbles of excitement for Charlie. "That makes sense. I hope you all enjoy yourselves."

Mrs. Johnson nodded as Charlie came bouncing into the room. "Ms. Carol! Did momma tell you what we're doing for my birthday?!" He didn't wait for her response. "We're going to Mouse and Cheese! Are you going to come too?!"

Mouse and Cheese was a popular kids arcade that served pizza. Philippa smiled down at him and shook her head. "I'm not, but I know that you guys are going to have so much fun."

Charlie's face fell. "But you have to come! Uncle Henry is coming!"

Philippa assumed her teacher position and prepared herself to calm him down, but Mrs. Johnson spoke, surprising Philippa. "You should come, Ms. Carol."

Philippa blinked in surprise; her teacher's smile failing her by sliding away in her shock. "I couldn't intrude."

"It's not intruding. You've become part of the family. It only seems right to have you join the celebration." Mrs. Johnson smiled, pulling Charlie close to hug him so they were both looking at Philippa with expectant faces.

Philippa opened her mouth to refuse so as not to step on anyone's toes, but paused. *I don't know. It feels like intruding. But she is insisting. However, it's probably not proper. It could be fun. I suppose it doesn't hurt.* "If you are certain you are alright with this."

"I wouldn't offer if I didn't mean it. And you can still have Friday off and just meet us there at five. I'll text you the address, and you can add it to your calendar."

Philippa bowed her head. "As you wish."

The Mouse and Cheese was flooded with kids and blinking lights from the arcade games. Philippa smiled as three kids ran past her to the playground set. She took several steps forward and to the side so as to be out of the way. She looked in every direction, her fingers playing around with the flowers she had embroidered on her light blue cotton shirt. *Where are the Johnsons?*

"Hello, stranger."

Philippa turned around to find Henry standing beside her. She smiled up at him, relieved to no longer be alone. "Good evening. Where are the others?"

"Running late. I was working on my friend's yard, and he lives just a few blocks from here, so I unsurprisingly arrived early. Come with me, I already got us a table in the party section."

Philippa followed behind him. The two walked through the arcade games all the way to the stage area where the animatronic animals were singing and dancing. Henry sat down at the table that was nearly in the center, a little plastic table card claiming the table as occupied, with the Johnsons' last name written in Sharpie on a blank square of the card. Philippa sat down, looking around at the world around them. It was crashingly loud. Kids were squealing and running, the animatronics singing loudly, and the games' sound effects sounded as though they were competing to see which was the loudest. A few years ago, this would have overwhelmed her, but after teaching for two years, Philippa enjoyed the noise.

"So, what did you do with your friend's garden?" Philippa asked.

Henry looked at her as he spoke, however his hands were busy folding a napkin. "He has a flower garden, but none of his buds have bloomed yet, so we spent the afternoon trying to figure out why."

"Did you figure out the reason?"

"Yep, there was root decay due to overwatering. I helped him figure out a watering system as well as work on having better drainage. This is the third problem that I've fixed this week that has to do with overwatering. How about you?"

"I don't think I've interacted with any overwatering problems this week."

"No, no. I meant what have you done today with your time off?"

Philippa smiled. "I called my sister, and we chatted while I did some cleaning, and she went grocery shopping."

"That sounds nice. Does your sister live far away?"

"Yeah, she lives in Massachusetts while she is finishing her medical schooling."

"What career is she wanting to go into?"

"Brain surgeon."

Henry's eyes widened. "That is rather ambitious."

"Yes, well it's a field of study that she really enjoys, and that means she puts her all into it. She has always loved dissecting the dead animals that we used to find in our dad's backyard."

"That sounds like Angela."

Philippa blinked in surprise. "Mrs. Johnson?"

"Yep. Angela used to be this very messy kid, but then she went to our grandmother's for two weeks when she was twelve and came back much more mature and put together."

"That's too bad."

Henry shrugged. "She was bound to grow up eventually. I think it was a plan our parents had, to make her a little lady, and then I would naturally follow her example and grow up. I'm pretty sure her throwing a squirrel onto the court during a basketball game had been the last straw."

"What?!"

"Ms. Carol!" Charlie ran over to Philippa and Henry, giving both of them a big hug.

"Sorry we came so late," Mrs. Johnson apologized, seating herself at the far end of the table.

"Annie took forever!" Charlie whined.

"Charlie, mind your manners," Mrs. Johnson scolded.

Annie sat down, in between her mother and Philippa. Mr. Johnson sat next to Henry, and Charlie sat at the head of the table. Mr. Johnson was smiling as he looked at his son, the ever-present exhaustion that followed him was nowhere to be found.

"Have you guys ordered yet?" Annie asked.

"Yep, I ordered a large pepperoni pizza with olives on it." Henry placed down his napkin, done with folding it.

Philippa looked at the napkin for several seconds before a burst of laughter broke through. The napkin was standing but tilted precariously, two flaps curling around the top in a deformed ear formation.

"Have you been trying to fold the napkin into a bunny?" Philippa asked, mirth coloring her voice.

Henry stared ruefully at his napkin. "Yes, I've been practicing since you taught the kids and me how to."

Philippa giggled as she shook her head at the napkin. Mr. Johnson raised an eyebrow, turning to his kids. "You two know how to make a napkin look like a bunny?" Charlie nodded enthusiastically, and Annie shrugged. "Do you two want to show your uncle how it's done?" He handed each kid a napkin from the dispenser.

Like magic, Annie came to life with excitement, and Charlie's eyes lit with joy. Both grabbed the napkins and began the process to fold a napkin. Annie paused. She grabbed two more napkins and placed them in front of her parents. At their look of confusion, she dramatically sighed.

"You guys have to make one too!"

"Oh, I don't know—" Mrs. Johnson began.

"Sure, we can!" Mr. Johnson declared.

Mrs. Johnson looked at her husband in astonishment but picked up her napkin and soon everyone, except for Philippa and Henry, was folding their napkins. Charlie finished first with Annie right behind him. Their napkins were a little derpy, but Philippa loved them. Mr. and Mrs. Johnson's were both a heap of folds.

"Hm," Mr. Johnson stared at his napkin. "That is harder than expected."

"That's okay, Ms. Carol can teach you."

The whole table turned to look at her. Philippa blushed at the attention but took a napkin. "It's really simple if you break it down to shapes." Philippa slowly took the table through the method of folding the napkin, keeping her instructions simple. By the time the pizza came, everyone had at least one napkin that semi-resembled a bunny. The pizza was eaten at a speed Philippa wasn't prepared for. Everyone was on their second slice by the time Philippa had finished discreetly pulling off the olives of her slice. *I suppose if I'm still hungry later, I could always eat leftovers in my fridge when I get home.*

"Let's go play the dance game!" Charlie declared after having his fill of pizza.

Everyone rose and followed the small boy as he made his way over to the dance game in the back of the arcade area. The game was a two-person game where you step on a certain tile to match the beat. The most intriguing part of the game was the floor. Every step you took on it, the floor would have light up colors, making small fireworks under your feet. Philippa watched in amazement as Annie and Charlie did the first round. Annie won, so she continued to the next level, pulling her dad on to play with her. Soon the two-player game had four people on it. It was magical. Not because of the fancy colors and electronics, but because of all the laughter. All four Johnsons were laughing, tumbling over each other.

"We should let them have some time alone together," Henry whispered to her.

Philippa nodded, and the two shuffled away, leaving the family to have fun together.

"What should we do first?" Henry asked, pulling a large bag of tokens out of his pants pocket once they were in the clear.

"You actually got tokens?"

"Of course. I was thinking I would challenge you to a game of hoops, but we can do something else if you're too scared."

"Are you baiting me?"

"That depends. Is it working?"

"Yes. Let's go find the hoops game and see if you're all talk."

"Ooh. You're getting into the spirit of competitiveness."

Philippa laughed and shrugged, putting her hands into her jean pockets. "It's not every day that I'm challenged to play hoops in a Mouse and Cheese."

"That's just sad. We need to broaden your horizons if you aren't challenged to hoops weekly."

The two arrived at the hoops game. Henry put in a token for each of them and the game began. Philippa laughed as she tried desperately to get the ball into the hoop but kept missing. She once overshot it so badly, it hit the top of the game and rolled into Henry's hoop.

"Thanks!" He laughed.

"Anytime."

Unsurprisingly, Philippa lost.

"Perhaps I do need to get challenged to hoops more often."

"Don't worry. We have the rest of the summer to fix your complete lack of coordination."

"Lack of coordination?!" Philippa squawked.

"Either that, or you thought the rules were to hit everything but the hoop."

"You chose hoops, I now challenge you to Tetris!"

"Tetris?"

"Yep."

"Is that the only game here you think you can beat me at?"

"No, I just know it's the fastest way to humble you."

Henry laughed, and Philippa's fake scowl melted and was replaced by a true smile. "Lead the way."

The two went through several different games, Philippa winning three and Henry winning five. They ended in the kitchen area, where the scent of pizza was absolutely intoxicating.

"All this winning has made me hungry," Henry said, strolling over to the ordering counter. Philippa went with him so that she wasn't awkwardly alone in the corner. *When Mrs. Johnson invited me to join them this evening, never in a million years did I imagine it would lead to me having a competition with her brother.*

"Hello, how may I help you?" The worker asked. She was a young woman, her brown hair pulled back in a ponytail and her bright red shirt stained with grease.

"Hi, I would like one slice of olive pizza, and one slice of pepperoni."

"Of course. Will that be everything?"

"Yes."

Henry paid and soon had two plates of pizza in his hands. He handed the pepperoni one to her, confusion on her face. *He must need me to hold this while he eats his other slice.*

"That's for you," he said, correctly interpreting her thoughts.

"Oh. You didn't have to."

"Sure, I did. I didn't even think earlier about how you might not like olives when I ordered olive pizza."

Philippa blushed in embarrassment. "You were perfectly fine to order olive pizza, everyone loved it. You didn't need to buy me a slice."

He simply shook his head as if this were a no brainer. "Then consider it my way of not eating alone. Come on, let's walk around and eat."

Philippa looked down at the pizza. "Thank you."

"Any time."

The two walked around, and Philippa's chest felt warm and fluttery as they talked and looked at the different games.

God, thank You for this day.

Chapter Twenty

"Stay close," Philippa told Charlie as he ran to look into one of the display windows.

The mall was crowded with people and red, white, and blue decorations. The Fourth of July was in a few days, and Mrs. Johnson had already let Philippa know that she and Mr. Johnson would be working. Philippa was happy to watch the kids since she didn't have any family nearby to celebrate with anyway.

"I don't get it," Annie grumbled, shuffling beside Philippa.

"What don't you get?" Philippa asked, standing on her toes to see over the crowd.

"Why are we at the mall if we're not going to buy anything?"

"Oh, we'll buy something. But for the majority, we're window shopping and enjoying the decorations. It's only once a year that the mall looks like this, and I want to enjoy it before it's all over. Charlie, you're going too fast."

The three of them stopped and looked at the window display of a thrift store. The window had large bunches of ribbon twirling around the edges of the glass, a large flag obscuring the view.

"Do you guys want to go in here?" Philippa asked, adjusting the pen that was holding her hair up.

"Why not?" Annie shrugged and led the way inside.

The three of them walked around, looking over the oddities that the store offered.

"Ms. Carol, what are we going to do for the Fourth of July?" Charlie asked, looking through the superhero action figures.

"Well, I was thinking we'd have a barbecue, but is there something specific that you two would like to do?"

"We can go to the park!" Charlie declared.

"No, we should go to the lake!" Annie exclaimed, surprising Philippa with her excitement.

"Yeah, the lake!" Charlie enthusiastically agreed, nearly knocking into a shelf.

Philippa adjusted her glasses as she considered the idea. *I suppose we could go to the lake. It's only half an hour away. I'm sure there is probably a great view of the fireworks too.*

"A barbeque lunch and then an evening at the lake it is then."

The kids whooped their excitement as they made their way out of the thrift store. The three walked around for a while longer, going into two more stores.

"Charlie, stay close by!" Philippa called to him for what felt like the hundredth time that day.

"Charlie, stop running around and giving Philippa a heart at-tack!" A deep voice called from behind her.

"Uncle Henry!" Charlie squealed, running past Philippa.

Philippa turned around and found Henry smiling down at Charlie.

"Hi, Uncle Henry." Annie nodded to him.

"Good afternoon, Henry," Philippa smiled at him. *What is he doing here?*

"Good afternoon. Annie messaged me a while ago that you guys were window shopping at the mall and that I should come."

Philippa raised her eyebrows and looked at the girl. "I see." Annie looked as innocent as a lamb, but Philippa wasn't buying it. *I'm reading too much into this. She probably just wanted to spend time with her uncle.* Philippa shook her head and turned back to Henry to find him staring at her. "You are more than welcome to join us. I was just about to make our way over to the food court for a quick snack, then go through a few more stores. Though we will probably go through stores on our way over to the food court."

"Sounds like a plan."

Annie and Charlie walked in front of Philippa and Henry.

"Were you working on another garden today?" Philippa asked, keeping her eye on Charlie the runner.

"No, I was helping a friend of mine pick flowers for their wed-ding."

Philippa was overwhelmingly aware of how close he was. With him standing beside her as he was, she could feel the warmth of his body heat, which made no sense to her since they weren't even touching. But if she moved an inch to get out of the way of a shopper, then their shoulders would brush, and she knew without a doubt that she would catch fire and explode into a million flames. *Lord, why am I so easily distracted by his proximity? Help me to keep myself focused on You.* Philippa, desperate to keep the mood light, fished around in her brain for something to add to the conversation. "Is that normally part of your job?"

"No, usually I provide florists with plants, so this was an exciting change to be on the other side of the counter."

"That's neat."

"Yeah, especially with the wedding theme. The couple chose Star Trek, so we went with really weird but interesting pieces."

Philippa stopped walking. "They chose a Star Trek wedding theme? That is so cool! Oh, my goodness, are they going to incorporate the uniforms by having the bridesmaids and groomsmen wear them?"

Henry's eyes widened. "You like Star Trek?"

"Of course, I do!" Philippa began walking again, going a little faster to keep up with the kids. Philippa scrunched her nose in embarrassment at an old memory, but quickly cleared it away.

"What is it?"

"What's what?"

"Whatever thought you had that made you look like you just ate a sour lemon."

Philippa's cheeks heated. "I don't know what you are referring to."

Henry laughed. "Oh yes you do. Come on, now I have to know. What about Star Trek could be making you this bashful?"

Philippa's shoulders lowered in defeat. "If you insist. It was when I was very young, and I didn't know I would regret it later." Henry leaned closer, intent on hearing her story. "When I was five, my dad dressed me up as Spock for Halloween."

Henry stopped. Seeing that the kids were still walking, Philippa lightly grabbed his wrist to drag him along. His wrist was warm, spreading heat through her just as she had suspected would happen. Philippa's cheeks felt like they were on fire. *Oh, this is so much worse than I thought.*

"Spock."

"Two years in a row," Philippa said, at a loss as to how to proceed. "I was young, my dad loved drawing funny eyebrows on me. It was a good way to connect with my dad." The truth was, Philippa was ashamed to admit that the Spock costume was her favorite due to the time with her dad as well as wearing her dad's favorite color. Just thinking of her dad sent a pang in her. *I wish I could spend the Fourth of July with him. It would be great to have him barbecue his awful hamburgers.*

"Philippa," she could hear the smile in his voice but refused to look at him. "You don't have to excuse your childhood costume. It's charming and tells me something that I didn't know about you."

Rather than calm down, Philippa's heart nearly exploded in anxiety and embarrassment. "And what did my costume from nearly twenty years ago tell you?"

"I thought it would be obvious. But if you can't figure it out, then I'll keep it to myself."

Philippa scrunched her nose at him. "I told you about my embarrassing memory, the least you could do is not leave me on the hook."

Henry shrugged and gave an evil chuckle. "I'm not as kind as you, so I don't feel bad for not letting you know."

"Well, that's just mean," Philippa grumbled, going on her toes to see the kids standing in front of a window display.

The window display that the kids were in front of had large blinking lights and flowers framing it. It was a lone table of dark wood with only two objects in it. By far, it was the plainest window they had stopped in front of, but Philippa felt it was perfect as she gazed at the picture of a man in dress blues, the folded and incased flag beside it glowing in the lights.

"Let's go inside," Philippa suggested.

The store was full of home décor merchandise. Pillows, paintings, vases, and kitchenware flooded the shelves from wall to wall. Philippa kept her eye on the kids while looking at the merchandise. The smooth glaze of a nearby glass vase shone in the overhead lights. Philippa studied the creation. It was pear shaped porcelain glass with intricate little flowers painted on it. A small bouquet of plastic flowers sat in it. Without much effort, she could see it sitting in the middle of her coffee table, the painted flowers matching the ones she drew. *But I don't need it.* Philippa smiled at it but moved on, shaking her head at Charlie who was trying unsuccessfully to climb Henry for a higher vantage point.

After making a full round of the store, Philippa bought Annie and Charlie large goofy patriotic top hats. At Henry's raised eyebrow, Philippa waved her hand through the air and laughed.

"We're going to have a barbeque; we have to look the part of crazy celebrators."

"So then why didn't you get one?"

"They only had two. I could have given myself one, but I decided the two of them look better with them than I ever could. It just adds some fun to the holiday."

"You're truly okay with working on your holiday?"

"Of course. It's not working if it's something you love, and I love these kids." Philippa smiled at the two kids who were several feet ahead of them, getting a sample at the pretzel stand. "I don't really have family nearby to celebrate Fourth of July with, so I am happy to get to celebrate with your family."

"I'm glad. With you there, I am sure we will have a fun Fourth. Though I will admit, I never pictured you as a goofy hat person."

Philippa giggled. "I'm a third-grade teacher; I have to add a little fun to everything, or else the world doesn't shine as brightly. It's the little things, like crazy hats, that make every day special."

"That does fit you. I should have known from the first day we met, and you made those napkin bunnies. Were you always this creative, or was it something you learned, or did somebody else show you?"

"I'm not sure," she adjusted her glasses. "I guess I had to take care of my younger sister all the time, so I always just made-up fun games or other things for us to do so we weren't bored all the time, and I guess that transferred over to my class."

"I bet you were a good older sister."

Philippa's heart warmed at the compliment. "I tried to be. I really tried."

"And from the sounds of your relationship with her now, you get to enjoy the reward of the hard work you put in."

"Yes. I think that's what so many people forget. It's hard to love someone all the time. It's hard to put so much effort into a relationship and not see the same amount of effort on the other side. Relationships of all kinds are hard, but working through it is what makes it so sweet." Philippa pondered the thought. If her parents had worked harder on their relationship, things would not be such a huge mess. Fourth of July wouldn't be so...lonely? *What am I talking about? I have Teressa, Charice, and the kids.*

"It's the price of sin: a never-ending amount of selfishness, so working to love another obviously goes so against our nature," Philippa continued.

"Once again, another reminder that the pursuit of Christlikeness is a battle worth fighting."

"Indeed, it is."

They reached the food court and got right to eating. With the strange hats as their only purchases, they decide to head home so they could plan out all that they wanted to do on the Fourth.

The sun was still strong and bright at five p.m. as Philippa pulled in behind Henry. Annie and Charlie hopped out of her car with their hats on, but Philippa sat for a moment in confusion as she stared at the third car in the driveway. *Why is Mr. Johnson here?*

She shook her head. *He must have come home early to spend time with the kids since he will be working on the Fourth.* Philippa smiled. *How kind of him.* Lately, he hadn't been coming home until after six, so it was unexpected for him to be here so early. She stepped out of her car and had to do a little jog to catch up with the kids and Henry, who were waiting for her by the front door.

"Come on, Ms. Carol!" Charlie's voice called. He was speaking loudly as though she were still in her car rather than a few feet away.

"Yeah, come on!" Henry called, his voice also piercingly loud.

It was against everything in her upbringing. Being loud for no reason would have made her mother cringe. But despite all of that, Philippa matched their volume, saying, "Almost there!" Then her steps slowed significantly.

Charlie ran over to her, his small hands grabbing hers. He pulled with all his might, but Philippa kept her gait slow as she strained against his force. Annie ran over and grabbed her left hand and pulled. With both of them pulling, Philippa stumbled a little but kept her step small.

"Pull, Charlie!" Annie said, pulling even more on Philippa's hand.

"Help us, Uncle! She's been put under a slow spell!"

"A slow spell?" Henry asked. He also came over to her. His evil grin made her nerves roar.

"You know, I think the spell is wearing off," Philippa's voice was squeaky as she quickened her steps. She would have run to the door, but now the kids were purposely blocking her path, mischievous grins that matched their uncle's were on their faces.

"Hmm, looks like it's still there." He was so close now, and his chuckle was low, reverberating from within.

Philippa turned just in time to see him charge at her. She squealed when he lifted her off the ground like she was a football. He opened the front door and all of them came in, laughing like crazy people while Philippa was clinging to his shoulders for dear life. They stopped in the entryway. All Philippa could see was the open door.

"Put me down! The slow spell is gone!" Philippa yipped.

"Oh, right!" Henry said as though he had forgotten that he was holding her. He gently placed her down and a deep voice behind her cleared his throat.

Philippa turned away from Henry to find Mr. Johnson staring at them. A blush of fire heated her cheeks. *Oh, my goodness. He probably thinks I am so unprofessional!* She quickly bowed her head to him. "Good evening, Mr. Johnson."

"Good evening, Ms. Carol. I am here, so I thought I would let you know that you can go home."

Philippa bobbed her head again. "Thank you, sir."

She turned to say goodbye to the kids, but Mr. Johnson stopped her. "One more thing. I know my wife and I said that we'd need you to watch them on the Fourth of July, but I will have the day off, so we have no need of you for that day."

Henry stiffened beside me. "Surely she can still come. She and the kids have already started making plans for the day."

"I'm sorry, but I would like to reserve the day for just our family."

"But she's family," Annie snapped. "She's been with us all day, most every day, for over a month. All of her family is out of state, she'll be all alone."

"Let her spend some of the Fourth with us," Henry tried reasoning, but stopped when Philippa put up her hand.

"I understand, Mr. Johnson." Philippa smiled. "It sounds like you all will have so much fun together. The kids and I can do our plans anytime, but you all should enjoy the time together."

Charlie ran over to her and wrapped his small arms around her legs. "But what about our silly hat party? You have to come."

She leaned down and gently pulled Charlie off her. "You all can do the crazy hats party without me. And," she ruffled her hand through his curls, "you are going to have so much fun. We can wear crazy hats any time. You go have fun with your dad."

Charlie nodded his head, but Philippa could tell he was still upset. Philippa grabbed her bag and went through the front door at a loss for what she could do to make the kids happy.

"We're going to watch the fireworks at the park." She could hear Mr. Johnson say as the door closed behind her.

"Will Mom be there?" Annie's usually strong voice wavered momentarily.

"No." Mr. Johnson's voice was quiet. He coughed and then said in a louder voice, "We're going to have fun, just the three of us, and Uncle Henry if he wants."

Philippa couldn't listen anymore. Her heart was shattering. She ached for the children and the pain they were going through, but she also could feel the ghosts of her own past brush and whisper to her. She couldn't go through a divorce again. It may not be her parents, but it felt like it did when her parents split.

Why? Why have You put me in this situation? I can't help them. I can't even help myself. The prayer was selfish, and she knew it. She couldn't possibly have all the answers all the time, but at that moment, she wished she did. She sat in her car's front seat and placed her hands on the wheel but didn't do anything to drive out. She just sat as memories flooded her. *Could I have stopped them from splitting?* Her parents had been happy a long time ago. She could see that joy in Angela and Horrace Johnson. In the moments where they set aside their differences and focused on love. She could see it. She had been hoping they could see it too. But she was wrong.

These kids that she loved so much were going to suffer the same fate she had. They would grow up lonely and never spend any holidays with family, because it was so hard to choose between them and not hurt any feelings. She didn't want that for them. She didn't want them to feel like they never had a home. But what could she do?

Pray. The thought came abruptly, but the more she thought about it, the more it made sense. *Dear Heavenly Father, please save this family. Please stop this separation. Guide Mr. and Mrs. Johnson to You, that their marriage would be a reflection of Your love. Please be with the children. Protect their hearts. May You save them from bitterness, and may they know You. Please work in me as well. Give me direction. May You shine through me and my actions and words. May You be glorified. Amen.*

It was barely a second after she finished her prayer when a knock on her car window made her jump. She rolled down her window as she peered at Henry.

"Sorry, lost in thought," she blushed. *How long have I been sitting here?*

"I'm glad. I was worried I missed you."

"Oh?" *What does he need?* "Did one of the kids forget something?" It was the only logical solution.

"No. I came out here to make sure you're okay."

Philippa blinked. *What did he say? Surely, I misheard him.* "I'm sorry. could you repeat that?"

"Are you okay?"

"Of course. Why wouldn't I be?"

"Because I saw how giddy you were at the mall. You were excited, and then Horrace just popped your bubble. You looked like a deflated balloon when you left."

Philippa smiled. She had never been compared to a deflated balloon. "Ah, well, I was just excited about the Fourth of July. But I'll be fine. I'll call Charice, and she and I will do something. It's better this way. Now the kids can spend the holiday with their dad. That's more important to me than crazy hats."

Henry sighed. "Yeah. It will be good for them to spend the holiday together, but I know the kids will miss you." He looked at the house for a moment but turned back to Philippa. "I'm sorry. I know that holidays must be lonely."

The previous sadness and frustration left her as a peace settled over her heart. "Actually, not really. There was a time long ago where it bothered me, but God has given me friends to help me. I never have to worry about being alone. Though sometimes, I let the idea of loneliness overwhelm me, like 'woe is me.' But that's just my selfishness winning. I am blessed with much love, and that's all I really need."

Henry grinned at her. "I'm glad. I guess I will see you on Wednesday."

"Yes!"

He stepped back, and Philippa drove home, her heart significantly lighter.

Chapter Twenty-One

Philippa looked at her reflection in the mirror. She was wearing a three-tiered dress of different patriotic fabrics and a dark blue ruffle going around her chest and arms to hold it all in place. With her flower crown of red, white, and blue, she felt a little childish. But she would be running late if she tried to change anything. So, she shrugged and grabbed her purse, heading for the front door of her apartment. Her hand scarcely touched the knob when a knock sounded. *That's odd. I told Charice I would meet her there.*

"Charice, you didn't have to—" She paused after opening the door. Instead of Charice, Henry stood with his hands behind his back, a smile settled on his face, however that half smile froze on him as his eyes widened. Those deep eyes softened though, as did the rest of his smile as he looked at her. "Oh." She self-consciously pulled her hair behind her ear. *Why is he here? Did Horrace get called in on an emergency? But then Henry would have the kids with him.* Philippa blinked, realizing she was being rude. She opened the door all the way. "Good evening, Henry. I would invite you in, but I was actually just heading out."

That snapped him out of whatever spell he was under. "Ah, yes, of course. I should be going as well, but I wanted to give you this before I forgot."

Philippa raised an eyebrow in surprise. "You don't have to give me any—" She stopped as he pulled out a glass vase of the most beautiful flowers from behind him.

Roses, lilies, and lupins swirled in great bouts of color. *I shouldn't take it.* But she couldn't stop herself from lightly touching the petals with the tips of her fingers. Henry caught her hand, his warmth radiating and blooming through her as he placed it onto the cool glass neck of the vase. Thankfully she had her grip on it because he let it go, leaving all the weight in her hand. She brought the vase closer to study it. The pear-shaped porcelain glass vase had tiny intricate flowers painted on it. She had seen this vase before. *It's the one from the mall. How did he know I liked it?* This close, the smell of the flowers flooded her senses, hypnotizing her with the intoxicating scent.

"I grew the flowers myself."

Philippa looked up from the flowers, embarrassed to have been so distracted by them. "You grew these?"

"Yes. I thought you might appreciate them. I hope you're not allergic to them."

Philippa mutely shook her head as she looked at them again. "They're beautiful. Thank you. You didn't have to. I don't want you to miss out on any of the celebrations."

"I wanted to." He took a breath and Philippa noticed his hands were shaking just the tiniest bit. *Is he nervous? Whatever for? I don't think I'm that scary.* "I also was wondering if you would like to go get dinner sometime. Maybe after watching the kids. Or some other day. Or even just coffee in the morning."

Philippa's heart stopped. "Are you asking me out on a date?"

He stood taller, and confidence rolled off him. "Yes, I am. Since the moment I nearly scared you to death, I've been intrigued by you. Your caring heart for the kids and for God is truly a sight to see. I would like to know you better."

Philippa's heart began beating erratically. *He thinks I'm intriguing.* She had thought fondly of him, but she had never dreamt that he would think twice about her. "I would love to go on a date with you."

Relief flooded Henry. "How does Saturday sound?"

"That sounds great."

"Perfect."

"Fantastic."

"Then I should let you go. I don't wish to keep you from your prior engagement." He bowed his head, copying what he had seen her do many times.

Philippa waved to him and watched him leave. When he was out of sight, she closed her door and slid her back down it, taking a seat on her white carpeted floors.

"Did that really just happen?"

She looked at the flowers as if they could answer. Butterflies were swarming inside her. She felt both like jumping and screaming for joy, as well as sitting and soaking it all in. She put her face in the flowers and inhaled deeply. Henry liked her. She was going on a date with Henry in less than a week. She could have sat there for hours but her phone went off. Philippa slid her thumb across the screen, answering without seeing who it was.

"Philippa?" It was Charice. "Are you almost here? I just pulled out the sparklers."

"Henry just asked me out!" Her cheeks were round and hurt from smiling.

"What?! Give me all the details!!!!"

So, she did, and Philippa rested in peace and joy as she got up and placed the flowers on her table, heading outside to drive to the firework show.

Chapter Twenty-Two

Philippa's heart was flying throughout the whole week. Thankfully, Henry was working on other people's gardens for a majority of the time. Every time he was near, her face erupted into flames even though she tried to keep her cool. *How do people go on dates so often? How do they not put themselves into an early grave?* It was a mystery to her, but she hoped the feeling never went away.

She hadn't given much thought to what the date would be like. She was too nervous to think about that. But somehow, Saturday had come in a flash, and she was left in bewilderment as to what attire was appropriate. It was eight in the morning, and he would be there to pick her up in an hour. So, in puzzlement, she did the logical thing and called the only expert she knew.

"Don't frown, you look lovely," Teressa sighed. They had been going through outfits for twenty minutes, and Teressa was multi-tasking between video chatting and making bread.

"I don't know. It feels like a bit much." She tugged lightly on her skirt. It was a nude pink circle skirt that fluttered around her and ended at her knees. Her shirt was white with eyelets to show her shoulders, small white delicate flowers fluttering off and across her shoulders and mid-length sleeves. It was something she had worn before, but suddenly it felt as though it was odd.

"You're being a silly worry wart. You look fine. Now, let's move onto shoes."

Philippa followed all her sister's instructions, choosing tan cord sandals that she tied around her ankles, reflective plastic butterfly earrings that dangled from her ears, and pulling the top half of her hair back with one of her decorative hair sticks. Her reflection was strange to her eyes. It was her, but now all she could see were the faults in the reflection. Her too straight hair, her chipped nail polish, and her shaking hands. *Oh, Lord. Look at me being so vain. I need to stop being so silly.*

The doorbell rang and Philippa looked at the clock on her nightstand. *It's time.* She rolled her shoulders back as Teressa gave her a thumbs up through Facetime and hung up.

Philippa opened her front door, nervousness, fear, excitement, and anticipation thrumming through her. Henry was standing there, for once wearing something other than a flannel. His brown polo looked freshly ironed and was paired with deep blue jeans. There wasn't a hint of dirt on his hands or jeans. Philippa grinned at him as he held his arm out for her.

"Good morning," She grabbed her purse, shut the door, and took his arm. His arm was warm, radiating heat that spread through her. She shook her head to try and focus on anything other than how close he was while he led her to his truck.

"Good morning. You look lovely."

Her cheeks warmed under his praise. "Thank you." He opened the passenger door for her, and she hopped in. By the time she was buckled, he was in his seat. "Where are we going?" She couldn't hide the anticipation in her voice.

"On an adventure."

"Everything with you is an adventure, I'm trying to figure out if today is going to be a good adventure or not." She pushed up her glasses.

"Oof," He chuckled as he turned the key in the ignition. "I'm flattered and hurt. But today is going to be a good adventure."

"Are you going to give me any clues as to what we're doing?"

"Nope."

Philippa smiled and shook her head. She normally liked to know what her day would look like, but she satisfied herself with the knowledge that no matter where they went, she would have fun.

"Oh!" She gasped in joy.

The farmers' market spread around her in great floods of people. The warm summer sun kissed her skin as she hopped out of the truck, too excited to wait for Henry to come around to open her door.

He laughed, the sound coming from deep within. "I don't think I've ever seen you jump, and here all I had to do was take you to a farmers' market to see you launch yourself like a cannonball. I hope that I've chosen our destination well."

Philippa jumped up and down a little as she nodded. "Yes! How did you know I liked the farmers' market?"

She put her arm through his and let him lead her to the vendors. "I asked Charice. She told me you love the farmers' market but don't get to go since you usually help out with the church food pantry on Saturday mornings."

"That's all she told you. She didn't tell you about how she got kicked out?"

They stopped to look at the first booth. This booth had different books and bookmarks, a familiar older woman sitting behind the table and smiling at them. *How do I know her?* Philippa scrolled through her memories before the face clicked into place.

"Mrs. Bear! How are you?"

Mrs. Bear's wrinkled face glowed as she smiled at Philippa. "Hello, dear. I am doing well. My son helped me clean out my basement, which hasn't been cleaned in the past twenty years, so now I have been selling different things here every week. This week is my book collection and the little crafts I've made in my spare time. My grandchildren came over last week, and they made me watch a marathon of fairy movies. I can crochet a lot while watching those movies."

"That sounds fun. I hope that you will still join us this winter to help with the school's choir. The kids love you, and it wouldn't be the same without your piano skills."

"Ah, you could replace me if you keep practicing. I do plan to help out this winter, but it will probably be my last year."

"That's unfortunate to hear." Remembering Henry was with her, she smiled and looked to him. He was listening with a polite smile but raised an eyebrow as she looked at him. "I'm sorry. My manners have evaded me this morning. Mrs. Bear, this is Henry; Henry, this is Mrs. Bear."

"Nice to meet you." He smiled at her, one of his charming ones that gave him a dimple in one cheek.

"You as well, young man. Are you taking our dear Philippa on a date this morning?" She twitched her eyebrows suggestively at him.

"Yes, I am."

"Philippa!" She admonished. "You are wasting a lovely morning and making a handsome man wait for your attention just to talk to an old hag like myself. Off with you! Enjoy yourself!"

Philippa's face heated. "Oh, you're not an old hag." She didn't dare say anything about a handsome man waiting for her attention. She knew she would burst into flames on the spot. Yes, Henry was handsome, but Mrs. Bear made it sound as though he were a puppy she had chained along.

"Pfft! Go! Off with the two of you!"

She shooed them away, and they both chuckled and followed her orders. The two walked past another table, and Philippa gave a light description of how she knew Mrs. Bear from the school's Christmas Caroling celebration they did every year.

"She has a true gift for music. She barely looks at the sheet music and yet somehow has it mastered. She is very kind, if a little overbearing."

"You paint a very good description of her. Do you know most everyone in this town?"

"A lot of them. When I was a kid, both of my parents lived in two different big cities. With the constant jumping around, it was hard to make good acquaintances. Once I moved out, I made a big effort at becoming one with the community."

"When I was a boy, my family lived in a small town like this one. But I was restless and thought that it was insignificant. I was unsatisfied with where God had placed me and tried to separate myself from them as much as I could. But seeing how this community flourishes together, I finally get it. A small town isn't miniscule, it's a big family."

"Exactly," Philippa grinned. "But what about where you live now? What's it like there?"

"Ah, it's a bigger city, so it's not so close knit. But in a way, it's very similar to here, because there are groups of people that work together. It's like a county of communities."

"Are you part of the community?"

"In a way. I think I'm part of more than one community. I go throughout the area and help where I can. But that leaves me spread thin, so it's hard to focus and connect on one specific place. I think about moving to somewhere smaller and less busy all the time."

"If you're looking for less busy, than you probably won't find it here. Throughout the winter we plan a bunch of projects and do as many fundraisers as we can so that in the spring and summer we can get as much done as possible."

"That is true. This place is very small but very mighty. And ambitious. I heard about the playground you guys are pushing to have built."

"Yes, well it's still in the planning stages. We're trying to make it accessible to those with disabilities, which is a bit harder than we first thought."

"If you guys are ever in need of landscape help, just give me a call. Or even just construction."

"You know construction?"

"Yep. My dad told me I could go into whatever field I wanted to as long as I had something to fall back on, so I got a double major in Construction Management and horticulture."

"That's neat. Where did you go to school?"

"A local community college. My parents said they would pay for my tuition if I lived at home. They were worried I'd get sucked into becoming a college frat."

"Yeah, I don't think I would like a frat Henry very much."

"That was their thinking too. I was upset about it then, but I've grown to really appreciate their help. What about you?"

"What about me?"

"Where did you go to college?"

"Oh, I got a really good scholarship for a university in Arizona. I stayed on campus, but I was known as the boring girl because I didn't want to party. What they didn't know was that I went to a party every week."

He missed a step and stumbled a little as they made their way to the next table. "You were a partier?"

Philippa's cunning grin grew across her face, making her eyes twinkle in mirth. "Of course. Every Sunday after church we had fellowship. If you think the club is crazy, then you're in for a surprise when college students get together to play For King and Country while eating boxes of pizza. It was always so loud and crowded."

"Wow, Philippa Carol, the elementary teacher, sounds like quite the riot."

Philippa laughed and shook her head. "College Philippa was. Now I watch kids and drink tea. A lot of tea."

Henry laughed as well. "That's true. I don't think I've ever known someone to drink so much tea in a day."

"Tea just happens to be the best drink ever created."

"How did you get so addicted to tea?"

"Addicted is a strong word." She let her fingers lightly caress a flower key chain.

"Strong but accurate."

"You have me there. I wish there was some great reason, like my grandmother used to give it to us on Christmas, or something else heartwarming, but the truth is that in college I drank tea for the caffeine. That one cup a day turned into seven a day during finals, and since then I've just had one with me everywhere I go."

"Hmm. Lackluster, but honest."

"Yep. And once I started playing sports, I learned the greatness of iced tea."

"What sports did you play?"

The conversation continued to grow as they both walked, learning more about each other while looking at knickknacks. By noon, Henry had bought Philippa a little crochet bumble bee, a pack of tea, and a fresh honey bun that they split. The sun streamed through the sky, its golden beams lightly coloring the few clouds that spotted the sky. The brilliance of the blue expanse was eye catching, a plane going past and leaving its line of combustion behind. Chatter hummed all around them, but they heard and saw none of it. The moment was almost as if time had stopped as Philippa giggled and put a hat on Henry, who was completely enchanted looking at her.

"Thanks for the fun," Philippa said. After five hours at the farmers' market, Henry said he had to get going soon to go to work, so they rushed Philippa home. Standing outside of her apartment door, Philippa wished that she could time travel to the beginning of the morning to relive it all over again. *I don't even know what I was so nervous about!*

"Thank you for spending the morning with me. Would you like to go on another date?" He was smiling down at her, but she didn't miss the small shake in his hands as he held the jar of honey for her.

Philippa nodded enthusiastically. "Of course. You already know my schedule."

A true-blue smile lit up his face. "I do. Until next time." He lightly put the honey into her hands. His hand barely touched her, but even the feather of the touch sent butterflies through her. Philippa smiled at him and watched him walk away. She waited until he was driving away before going into her apartment. She placed her new things on her kitchen table, beside the vase of flowers that were still fully bloomed. With her kettle heating up some water, she spun onto the couch.

She had scarcely taken a breath when her phone started ringing. She looked to see four missed calls, all from the same person, so she decided to answer the phone.

"Hi, Charice."

"Girl!" Her voice pierced through the speaker. "How was your date?!"

"It was—" Philippa paused as her kettle let out its screech. She quickly took the water off the heat and placed the phone on speaker as she began to get her new tea steeped.

"It was that bad that you screamed?!"

"What? No. That was my kettle."

"That's a relief. So how was it?!"

"It was..." She paused to find a word to describe the day. "Wonderful," A dreamy sigh slipped out.

"Ooh! Give me all the details."

Philippa settled onto her couch, her phone in one hand, her tea in the other. "Well, it started with outfit number thirteen..."

Chapter Twenty-Three

Sunday morning, Philippa still felt like she was flying. Everything seemed so much brighter as she walked through the front doors of the church. Charice, at her usual desk, waved and called her over.

"Good morning," Philippa said as she pulled her hair behind her ear.

"What's behind your back?" Charice asked, skipping pleasantries.

"I don't know what you mean," Philippa angled herself so the item in her hand was better hidden behind her.

"Philippa, please, the curiosity will be my end," she threw her hands onto her heart for effect.

Philippa laughed and finally showed the treasure. Charice gasped, "Is that what I think it is?!"

"Yep. Coffee from your favorite café across town."

Charice snatched the cup from Philippa's grasp and held it close. "Oh! Thank you! But you didn't need to go all that way for little old me."

"I wanted to. I woke up early this morning, and I didn't want to bake, so instead I went on a drive."

"You drove that far?"

"I had a lot to think about, and the drive was nice and predictable."

"Were you thinking about McDreamy."

Philippa blushed at the nickname for Henry. "Shhhh! Someone's going to hear you, and then it will go all around town."

Charice took a sip of her coffee and hummed in delight. "Have you heard from him since we last spoke?"

"No, but I'm pretty sure he'll be here today."

Something behind Philippa caught Charice's eye, and whatever it was gave her a start as she actually put down her coffee.

"What's wrong?" Philippa asked before turning around and coming to a halt as she looked at the five people that entered the church.

Mr. and Mrs. Johnson strolled in with bright smiles on their faces, dressed in their Sunday best as Charlie raced over to Philippa in his jeans and clean blue shirt.

"Ms. Carol!" He cheered as he flung himself into her arms.

Annie, in a denim skirt and cream shirt walked over to Philippa as well. "Hello!" Philippa exclaimed, shocked to see the family there.

Henry laughed and kept in step with Mr. and Mrs. Johnson, though he smiled at her. "Good morning, Philippa and Charice," he nodded to Charice.

"Good morning," Philippa said through her grin.

"I decided to bring the rest of my crew for today."

"I see."

Mrs. Johnson lightly tapped her brother's arm. "Don't be silly. It's a beautiful day, and the kids have been asking to come to church, so we thought we would try to make it here on time."

"Yes, Charlie and Annie made sure I was ready in a timely manner," Mr. Johnson chuckled as he rubbed the back of his neck.

Philippa smiled down at the kids, "Aw, how fun."

Charice, being the good Church Welcomer that she was, snapped into the conversation. "Hello, Johnson family. It's so lovely to see you all today. The service will be beginning in ten minutes, but until then we have loads of treats and refreshments. This week is a regular church service, but next week we are having a pot-blessing. We would love to have you join us then, I can assure you, we will fill you all to the brim with food."

Mrs. Johnson beamed at Charice, "That sounds lovely. I will add it to my calendar."

Mr. Johnson, not seeming to have heard any of this, squinted at Charice. "I recognize you."

Philippa's heart stopped. *Oh, dear. Please let him not be upset that she's been the thorn in his side at work!* Charice, not even pausing, nodded. "Yes, I am the Business Intelligence Analyst that's been giving you notes on your project for the past month and a half."

Understanding lit Mr. Johnson's eyes, and his smile stiffened. "Ah, yes, now I remember."

"Though, I try to keep work at work, I must say that I am highly invested in this project. I can see this medication truly helping a lot of people."

Surprised, Mr. Johnson blinked. "Oh?"

"Yes. That's why I have been so involved. This can help a lot of people, so I want it to have the best chance for success."

"You do?"

"Of course. But as I won't waste your time any longer, why don't you all go enjoy the refreshments."

The kids rushed over to the snack table, and Mrs. Johnson followed close behind them. Philippa joined Henry on the side to watch the family as Mr. Johnson stayed by the front desk. *What is he doing?*

"Ms. – I'm sorry, I don't remember your last name," he started.

"Oh, you can just call me Charice." She smiled at him before taking a sip of her coffee, only briefly flicking her eyes to Philippa.

"Well, Charice, I owe you an apology."

Philippa, fiddling with the red pen that she brought everywhere, dropped her pen. Mrs. Johnson, across the room helping Charlie get a croissant, straightened abruptly. Charice, ever the professional, kept her open expression and didn't look at all phased.

"An apology?"

"Yes. Since the moment you were brought on, I have been against you and have said some unkind things about you. I believed you were trying to cause problems so you would stay on longer and get a bigger pay out, but I was wrong. I'm truly sorry."

Charice nodded. "I can understand how I have upset your work, but I thank you for the apology."

Mr. Johnson smiled. "I truly am sorry. If you are ever in need of assistance, you know where to find me. Now if you will excuse me, I think I shall go join my wife and kids before the service begins."

Charice grinned. "Of course. I hope you and your family have a lovely day."

Mr. Johnson tilted his head in acknowledgement before turning to his family, taking his wife's outstretched hand.

Philippa stood in shock, letting Henry lead her over to Charice. "Did that just happen?" Charice whispered, her voice so light Philippa could barely make out the words.

"I think so?" Philippa pushed her glasses up her nose.

"How?" Charice asked.

Both girls turned to Henry who merely shrugged. "He and Angela were talking this morning about perspectives, but that's all I know."

"Well," Charice took a sip of her coffee, "God is choosing to bless me in so many different ways today."

Philippa laughed and patted her friend's hand. "We should be heading inside."

The three filtered through the doors, the Johnsons following behind after a moment or two, frosting lining Charlie's cheek.

Philippa and Charice sat together, but Henry and the Johnsons sat in the row behind them. The sound of them singing together filled Philippa with gratitude as she marveled at all that could happen in one morning.

Chapter Twenty-Four

The next two weeks seemed to fly by in seconds. Henry had become the chauffeur for all the outings Philippa took the kids out on. The four of them went to museums, hiking trails, and the aquarium a few towns over. Henry had bought face paint, while Philippa and Charlie made posters for Annie's first soccer game. They looked a little crazy, going all out for a children's game of soccer, but Annie's smile made it all worth it. Philippa still fondly remembered falling asleep on the couch with Charlie on her lap and Annie's head on her shoulder while watching a movie after the game.

She and Henry had gone on two more dates since that first one. One was a quick coffee date between his jobs, and the other was bowling, where they had learned, much to her embarrassment, that Philippa was terrible at bowling. Of course, Henry had also taken Philippa and the kids to lunch every Wednesday and Friday. It was all like a dream. A dream that Philippa never wanted to end.

It was the last week of July, and Philippa was setting everything up for their Friday game night. The dining room that had seemed so imposing when she had first arrived was now familiar and welcoming. The wooden table held the cards, the matching chairs holding the kids and Henry. Philippa smiled while listening to Charlie giggle as Henry pretended Charlie was invisible.

Thank You, God. Thank You for the joy that You have given me. She was filled with love for the people around her, but it was also bittersweet as she knew she had to give an answer soon about her teaching abroad program. *I don't want to lose the kids. But then again, they were never mine to keep. I am just so confused. I've felt called to missions for years, and now that the opportunity has arrived, I'm conflicted.* She didn't even let herself look at Henry. She already knew he was one of the biggest complications to her plan. *Why did I say yes to a date when I was planning on leaving? Anything that happens between us can't last. Unless he's willing to wait. No. I can't make him wait for me. I need to tell him tomorrow. He deserves to know that I may be leaving.* With that decision made, Philippa put the stress away and focused on dealing the cards.

Charlie won the first round. He was loudly letting the world know his victory when Mr. Johnson came in. Mr. Johnson, usually pristinely kept, had his coat off and his hair messily windswept. Philippa stood from her spot.

"Good evening, sir. We were just playing some Dutch blitz."

Charlie jumped to his father. "Dad! I won! You wanna play?!"

Philippa was completely prepared for him to say no. She was thinking of how best to comfort Charlie when Mr. Johnson took her completely by surprise and nodded.

"Sure, son. Although, it's been quite some time. You will probably have to remind me of the rules."

Philippa was still standing rigid with shock as the two sat down and Charlie explained all of the rules.

"Here, Philippa." Henry lightly took the deck from her hand, breaking her out of the trance. "I'll deal this round."

"Oh, I should probably get going. I wouldn't wish to intrude on family time."

"You can stay, Ms. Carol," Mr. Johnson said. "If you wish. You wouldn't be intruding."

Philippa blinked but sat. Henry dealt the deck, and Philippa didn't have any time to dwell on how odd Mr. Johnson was acting, because once the game started, all anyone could do was try and win. Annie won the next round, Henry after that, and then Mr. Johnson did. Philippa had never heard so much laughter in the dining room. When Mrs. Johnson came in, Philippa could have jumped up and down and screamed her delight as Mrs. Johnson joined in the game.

Mrs. and Mr. Johnson were absolutely lethal in their banter.

"Thank you for playing right into my hands," Mrs. Johnson said after Mr. Johnson placed an eight down. She slammed down a nine and quickened her search for a ten.

"No, thank you," he said, ramming down the ten.

Mrs. Johnson stuck her tongue out at him. *Mrs. Johnson stuck out her tongue!* Philippa couldn't get over the change in her employers. She had never seen them like this. Annie and Charlie's faces were caught in bright smiles that brimmed with joy, Henry was grinning at his sister, and Philippa felt a peace settle over her. *Lord, please heal this marriage. Please bring them back together.*

Philippa pulled away from the table after Charlie had won for the fourth time. "Alright, I better head home, but you all have fun."

Charlie and Annie barely paid her any mind. A small part of her missed the hugs they would give her when she left, but she much preferred for them to have this time with their parents.

"I'll walk you to the door," Henry said, rising as well.

She smiled at him and waved goodbye to everyone else, who were all too absorbed in their game to notice. Philippa and Henry wordlessly went to the door, where Philippa slipped on her shoes and grabbed her purse. Ready to go, she stood straight up and faced Henry. He was closer than she had expected, only a few inches away. She could feel heat radiating from him, warm like a summer sun. She blushed at the close proximity. *I'm being silly. Mr. Johnson has stood this close before.* But there was a world of difference between Henry and Mr. Johnson, the first one being that only one could make her blush this often.

Henry was looking down at her, a small smile across his face. His eyes were locked on hers, and she suddenly found it very hard to even think. *I need to get out of here. Whatever spell I'm under cannot continue until after he knows about the teaching abroad thing.* "I, ummm." She took a breath in a desperate attempt to remember how to speak clearly. "I should be going."

Henry nodded, his eye not leaving hers. "Are you free tomorrow?"

"Umm, yes, wait, maybe. I mean, yes, I am free for most of the day." She adjusted her glasses. "I have to help out at the church at six in the evening. We're setting up for a big potluck."

"Then may I take you to lunch?"

"Of course." She didn't even try to ask where to. She had learned that he had immense joy in surprising people. *Lunch. Lunch is good. That's the perfect time to tell him.* She pulled the stray hair that had fallen from her bun behind her ear. "I'll see you then."

"I'll be there at eleven-thirty."

Philippa nodded and lightly turned the door handle. It hung open for several moments as Philippa and Henry continued to stare at each other. A cold breeze fluttered past them, reminding Philippa about where she was and what she was doing. "Right. Good night."

"Good night." He held the door open for her and didn't close it until he saw she was safely in her car.

Once the door closed, and she couldn't see him, Philippa sighed. She pulled the pen from her hair, and her bun untwirled to fall around her shoulders. She felt warm, and her lungs were doing something strange as it was hard to breathe. "I should have just told him right then and there." *But then I probably wouldn't get to go on a date with him tomorrow.* It was terribly selfish. She liked him. A lot. "It doesn't matter if I want it to last a little longer. He needs to know."

But even as she pulled out and began her drive home to her tiny, lonely apartment, her courage began to crumble. *Please give me the strength I need, Lord. I'm so scared, and I don't want to lose him. But I still feel this call to go.* Like a tug on her heart, she could see all the kids that had stared at her in the pictures she was sent every month. Those kids needed someone, and she knew she could help them. She could tell them about the God of the universe. But she would leave the smiles she had come to love here.

Chapter Twenty-Five

Philippa adjusted the yellow tule bow that secured the back of her hair. She had pulled the front layers of her hair back, the rest hanging down in loose curls that she knew would further deflate as the day went. The yellow sun dress fluttered around her as she waited beside the front door. It was nearly time for Henry to pick her up, and she was completely ready. Her white tennis shoes were tied and pristine, her daisy earrings dangled from her ears, and her small pearl bracelet was secured to her left wrist. She felt like a bundle of summer, but Teressa had said that she looked perfect when Philippa messaged her a photo of the outfit. She was physically ready for the date, but mentally, she was anything but ready. *How am I going to tell him? What if he decides to break things off?* She desperately didn't want to lose him, but she couldn't keep stringing him along. *He needs to know. It's better to let him know now than later when it's too late.* The thought made sense but didn't ease or comfort her at all. *I need to think of something else, or I'm going to be a sweaty mess when he gets here.*

I wonder where we are going. Because it was lunch time, her best guess was a quick bite before he had to go to his next job. They would go to some local diner; they would make the usual small talk that began every conversation, and then she would break the news. Simple. Easy. If only it was as easy and straight forward as that. She felt queasy, and her nerves threatened to undo her. *Dear Heavenly Father, please steady me. Guide my words and actions. May this all be to Your glory. Amen.*

A knock on her door made her jump but smile as she opened it. "Hello, Henry." She didn't look at him until she had stepped out of her apartment and had the door closing behind her.

He was wearing a blue polo and jeans, freshly ironed and smelling like detergent. *He must not have had a job this morning.* He smiled at her. "Hello." He tilted his head to the left. "My truck is just this way."

She put her arm in his and let him lead her there. Soon, they were buckled in, and Henry was turned to her as he guided the truck out of the parking lot. "Any guesses as to where we are going?"

"A diner."

"Nope."

"A bowling alley so you can see my lack of skill in that sport again."

"Good idea, but no."

"Then I'm not sure." She lightly shrugged.

A wicked smile made its way onto his face. "Fantastic."

Philippa smiled as she shook her head at him. She opened her mouth to respond when he pulled into a parking spot. They had parked at one of the construction sites. She couldn't remember what was being built at this spot, but the whole area had a fence with a tarp over the walls with brand logos on it, so she couldn't even peek to figure it out.

"What are we doing here?" She asked.

"Surprise. This is where we are having lunch."

"You want to look at logos while eating lunch?"

"No, we're not eating specifically here. We're going in there." He gestured to the fence.

"Umm, I don't think we're supposed to go in there."

"I have permission for us to eat lunch here. This is one of the projects I've been working on."

"Oh. Okay then." She hopped out of the truck and followed Henry past the tarped fence. The moment she could see past the logos, she stopped and let the view sink in. Lucious green grass, spread around, glowing in the sun. Large bushes that were waist high opened a path for them to follow.

"Whoa."

Henry smiled at her reaction. "The city wanted a floral garden to use for events and enlisted my help. Follow the path."

Philippa blinked but did as he said. Amongst the evergreen bushes were flowers. Purple, pink, yellow, and a rainbow of other colors delighted her eyes. She let her fingers glide lightly against the leaves as she continued down the twisting path. The maze eventually ended with a stone path, which she followed to a wooden arch with pink roses twirling around the wood panes. Philippa walked through the arch and again stopped in her tracks to find a blanket of food in front of her. Fruit and bread stood in the wooden basket that sat in the corner, plates beside it.

"Oh my," she gasped.

"Do you like it?"

"It's incredible."

"I'm glad that you think so." He lightly grabbed her wrist, his fingers a soft warmth to her. He pulled her to the picnic blanket, which was good because she was just too distracted by all the beauty around her. She sat across from where Henry was sitting, tucking her knees beneath her. He pulled sandwiches out from the basket as well as strawberries. She took hers gratefully and bowed her head as Henry quickly prayed over the food.

"So, how did you get away with this?" she asked after taking a bite of the egg salad sandwich on sweet white bread.

"I held the boss at gun point, and he told me I could."

"Hm, so I'm a dating a violent man. This doesn't look good for me," she chuckled.

"No, it was a water gun at the company picnic two weeks ago. And he had said no."

"Ah, so we really are breaking and entering," Philippa said calmly. She knew that he had permission to be here. It was strange, she had only known Henry for a short while, and yet she knew he wouldn't go against his supervisors' wishes. She knew his moral character. She knew him. *How strange of an idea. I never thought that I would get to this point. I had never even considered that I would become so attached to a person. But here he is.* Philippa had seen the struggles of maintaining a marriage. She didn't want to end up like her parents, or the Johnsons, where there is love but so much hate layering over it. *Do I even know how to work through a relationship?* But Henry was making her believe it was worth the risk. Worth the work to keep a marriage together.

"As interesting of a date as that would be, no. I begged every day for two weeks, and he finally relented." Henry declared, pride lining his tone.

"Why did you fight hard to have a picnic here? Not that I'm complaining, I'm happier than a tweety bird about this place, but it seems like a lot of work for you."

"I knew you would like it and appreciate this place. You don't have a lot of spare time, but I really wanted to show you some of my work. What better place than here and now to show you what I've been spending a portion of my summer on?"

Philippa smiled. "You truly are gifted."

"Thank you."

Philippa took a breath, the sweet floral air filling her lungs. Her heart twisted as she mustered the strength she needed. *He needs to know now.* "Henry, I have something I need to tell you."

He paused and looked to her, his eyes locking on hers. Her nerves felt like they could explode at any moment, and yet he looked cool as a cucumber. "Yes?"

"I, um. I may be leaving for a trip in a few months." *There. I've said it.*

"A trip?"

"Well, a little more than a trip. I have been given the opportunity to teach abroad in a mission field in China. If I go, I'll leave in June for a training and then head out to China in July. I would be gone for at least a year."

He was silent, the space between them becoming oceans of distance. "I see. So, you haven't made your decision yet?"

She mutely shook her head. "I keep going back and forth."

"Well," He blew out a breath. "Charice said that you've been dreaming about this for a long time. Why are you hesitating?"

"You spoke to Charice about this?"

"Of course. Both Charice and Mrs. White cornered me a few Sundays ago, when they realized I was interested in dating you. They warned me of a few things, one of them being that you would be leaving."

"And yet you still asked me out? Why?"

"Because I knew you were someone I could fight with."

"You want to fight?" She blinked.

"No, no, no. Not that kind of fight with. You may be small, but you're a teacher. You could totally take me down." Philippa laughed. She could never in a million years beat this large gentleman. He smiled at her laugh, his expression softening. "I meant you were someone that would fight along with me. We'll fight together and for each other."

"That is. Well," she blushed. "it's a lot to take in."

"You never did answer my question." He leaned in slightly, making alarm bells ring in her head. *Surely, it's illegal for him to be this close.* He was still a polite distance from her, but that didn't change that she could inhale the earthy scent that always followed him, and it was doing something silly to her brain.

"Hm?"

"If you have dreamed about this mission work, why are you hesitating?" he asked, snapping her out of her haze.

"That's a good question." *It's one I've been trying to answer for a while now,* she thought bitterly to herself. "I guess I'm afraid."

"Missions are hard."

"That's just the thing. I'm not afraid to give up all my possessions. To go hungry, to be under threat of attack. I know God will give me the strength I need. But I'm afraid of losing these close relationships I've cultivated. I've made my strongest connections here. Charice, Mrs. White, **you**. What if I can never make such close friends ever again? What if I'm unlovable, and I have somehow duped everyone around me into thinking I am lovable?" She hadn't realized she was crying until after her confession, the tears stinging her cheeks and the corners of her eyes. "I'm sorry. I shouldn't be dumping all of this on you." *Especially when you've made such a beautiful picnic.*

"Philippa, you can talk to me anytime. And you know that you are loved beyond imagination. Jesus Christ died for you. His blood is the ink to the love letter addressed to you. I'm sorry you have been carrying this weight for so long." He shifted slightly and pulled a piece of paper from the back of his jean pocket. He unfolded it and handed it to her.

The white lined paper crinkled in her shaking hands as she read the list of names that ran twice the length of the page, all names of her community members. "What is this?" she asked.

"This is a list of all the people that gave me a talking to before I could ask you out. They are all people who threatened to visit many horrors upon me should I break your heart. I didn't have any way to contact your father, so I had Charice make a list of the people that considered you family so I could ask them all for permission to ask you out."

Philippa blinked rapidly. "You asked all these people?" *This is nearly three fourths of the town! Why would he go through this much effort?*

He nodded and lightly wiped a tear from her face, his warmth taking away the cold of her tears. "I wanted to do it right, and they all consider you family. They all love you. No matter where you go, people will love you. And when you're ready to return, there will be a long line of people ready to welcome you back. I will be second in line."

"Second?"

"Charice told me if I got in between the two of you, she would shove a clove of garlic up my nose."

Philippa giggled, a small tinkling sound that grew into real laughter. "Thank you."

"You're welcome." He sat back, bringing a more comfortable distance between them, though Philippa was acutely aware of the lack of his warmth. "Philippa, I meant it. If this is what God is calling you to, I want to encourage you. I think that what we have is special, but God's plan is better than my feelings. I will wait for you, if you will let me."

Philippa's heart soared as she felt like she could melt into a puddle. "I don't even know if I'm leaving." She raised her hand to further emphasize her point, but Henry caught it midair, his warmth again encircling her.

"Then," he started, his eyes glued to hers, and she found hers magnetized to his as well. "Let's continue our picnic and deal with it when it comes."

She nodded, finding herself unable to speak. A butterfly, its wings of orange and black, fluttered onto their joined hands. Philippa pulled her eyes from his and watched the small insect flap its wings. Just as suddenly as it had come, it flew into the air. The butterfly fluttered around, and Philippa laughed as it matched the enthusiasm of the butterflies inside of her. She smiled down at the list of names Henry had given her. *No, not a list. A family tree.*

CHAPTER TWENTY-SIX

Philippa and the kids entered the house that Tuesday in a loud burst of laughter. They had spent the morning shopping for school supplies for the new year. It was crazy to Philippa that the summer was nearly over. She was excited about the possibilities the new school year possessed but also nervous about the change in schedule. What would her new students be like? However, school shopping always brightened her mood. The colorful pencil boxes, the grammar posters, and the bright backpacks always made her smile.

Unfortunately, their laughter was short lived as the sound of yelling reached Philippa's ears.

"You put your stupid job before this family!" That was a female voice.

"I am trying to save lives!"

"No, you're looking at a computer all the time. You don't even know what it's like to hold someone's hand while they are dying!"

"I'm working to find a solution where they don't die!"

"Then where are those solutions? Where's that cure to cancer?! Nowhere! You put your job before the kids for nothing. Before me for nothing!"

Philippa and the kids stared in horror at Mr. and Mrs. Johnson in the living room having a screaming match. Mrs. Johnson, seeing them in her peripheral vision, paused and looked at them. "Annie, Charlie, go up to your rooms and put away whatever is in those bags. Your dad and I are just going to continue our discussion."

Annie and Charlie mutely nodded and went upstairs with downcast eyes.

"Ms. Carol, my husband and I are home for the rest of the day, so you are free to go," Mrs. Johnson said between gritted teeth.

Philippa bobbed her head and turned to leave, freezing when Mr. Johnson sneered, "You make yourself sound like a saint, but you only picked up more days a week after I gave you the divorce papers."

"I needed a way to afford caring for myself and having a place for the kids to stay when they're with me."

"Oh, please. You just wanted to hide from the kids so they don't ask questions."

"How dare you! I at least love our children!"

Philippa gasped in horror. "Mr. and Mrs. Johnson!"

Mrs. Johnson breathed in deeply before turning to Philippa. "Ms. Carol, we told you that you can go home now."

What do I do? I can't let this get worse. "Yes, I understand and thank you, but please let me take the kids out."

"Why?" Mr. Johnson pulled back and furrowed his brows at her.

"I think it would be good for them," Philippa said vaguely. Mr. Johnson kept his hard stare on her until the truth spilled from her lips. "I don't wish for the children to hear your words that are spoken in anger."

"Ah," Mrs. Johnson nodded.

"Do not worry yourself. We will continue this conversation at a later time," Mr. Johnson huffed, throwing himself onto the couch.

"Our conversations are not your business, either," Mrs. Johnson narrowed her eyes.

"You hired me to take care of your children's physical and emotional wellbeing. If they heard what you just said, they would be torn apart," Philippa said before she could stop herself. Once she started, Philippa couldn't hold herself back any longer. "They are already going through a lot, and they probably heard every word you said. If you keep going, you may create more damage than can ever be fixed."

"Our kids are fine. Our priority right now is getting through this divorce as smoothly as possible." Mrs. Johnson replied, leaning her back against the wall as Mr. Johnson returned his attention to them after realizing the conversation wasn't over.

"I believe that you two have a responsibility to be there for your family."

"Excuse me?" Mrs. Johnson asked, her voice losing its anger and turning to something much more hollow.

"You made a commitment to this family when you got married and had a child."

"You're making it sound like we're abandoning them," Mr. Johnson straightened, his defensiveness hardening his expression.

"I don't mean to make you feel bad. I just want you both to understand what you're doing."

"And what do you think we're doing?" Mrs. Johnson hissed.

Philippa took a breath and uttered the words she prayed she wouldn't regret later. "You're putting yourselves before your kids." The words hung in the air for a moment. Philippa continued, hoping to get through to them to see the damage they were doing. "You are both gone all of the time, and you don't have to be. And when you are home, you're shouting at each other. The kids have had to find ways to drown out the noise. They hide and feel alone all the time. The people they love most are about to separate permanently."

"It's better for them if we separate." Mr. Johnson sighed, the fight leaving him.

Philippa took a tentative step towards them. "I adore your family. I just don't want to see it end up how mine did. I don't even talk to my parents anymore. My parents gave up on fighting for each other, and so they reasoned that it would be best to just split. But I've seen the two of you when you're with the kids." A smile lilted her voice. "You both have fights in you, for certain, but you love each other and your kids. Why don't you both use that fight in you to fight for each other?" Henry's words passed through her lips, and for a moment she marveled as they solidified and became her own. You can fight for love. Fighting isn't the end, it's the pursuit.

"There are times when you two are going to have problems and will hurt each other, but you must have grace."

Mrs. Johnson's eyes watered, and Philippa felt hope flutter in her heart until Mr. Johnson gave a bitter laugh. "No. We loved each other many years ago, but there is no way to salvage this relationship. You need to leave."

He ran his hands through his hair in exasperation.

Philippa, sensing she'd gone too far, nodded. "I'll see you next week."

"No, you won't," Mrs. Johnson snapped. "If you're spewing such silliness to us now, then you must be doing the same to our children. Filling their heads with nonsense to turn them against us." Her voice was getting louder and louder. "Get out of my house and stay out. I don't want you to even look at my children again!"

Philippa took a step back as everything in her froze. "Y-your firing m-me?" She stammered.

"You heard her," Mr. Johnson grumbled. "Now leave."

A calm came over her. Fired. She took a breath and bobbed her head to each of them. "If that is what you wish." Anger bubbled around her, but she swallowed the feeling down. "It's been a pleasure to work for you. Your children are lovely. No matter how this ends, I will be praying for you."

With her purse already on her shoulder she left the house, aware of the eyes on her as she exited. As soon as the door closed behind her, her legs began to tremble. What have I done?

"Pip!" Annie called from the second floor.

Philippa turned to wave, but Annie and Charlie were already hopping down to run to her. Philippa's only thought as they crashed into her in a hug was, they must have heard. Annie and Charlie cried into her arms, their tears turning into sobs. Annie pulled back for a moment, her crying turning into an empty hollow look.

"They really are destroying everything," she said bitterly, her eyes not focusing.

"No," Philippa brushed the hair out of Annie's face and made her look at her. "Listen to me. Your parents love you. They aren't trying to hurt you. I know it's going to be a hard time for a little while, but don't forget, Jesus loves you. If you accept Jesus Christ as your savior, then you will become a child of God. He died for you." Annie nodded, tears springing in her eyes again, her eyes scrunching in emotion. "Teach your brother all that you've learned. And show love to your parents. They need it."

"I don't think I can," Annie sobbed.

"Then pray for them. I will forever have you in my prayers." She pulled them close and gave them one last squeeze. "I love you both."

She pulled back and walked away, tears in her eyes as she got into her car. What have I done?

Chapter Twenty-Seven

The setting sun would have been a beautiful sight to behold if Henry hadn't been in such a rush. His hands itched to be unrooting the problem that Annie had alluded to through a text he'd found on his phone after work. The typed words still glowed in his memory.

Super big prob. Get to the house a.s.a.p.

A big problem. He didn't like the sound of those words. Philippa hadn't messaged him yet, which also concerned him. If there was a problem with the kids, she usually gave him a head's up. But not today. The lack of a message made him even antsier. If he didn't have equipment in the back of his truck, he would be speeding to the house, regardless of the possibility of a ticket. He needed to know what was wrong.

"Annie, why couldn't you just spell out the problem?" he muttered as his fingers rapidly tapped the steering wheel while waiting for the light to turn green.

It was another five minutes before he swerved into his usual spot on the driveway. He jerked the keys out of the ignition of the car. The air smelled of smoke, but nothing lethal, more like one of the neighbors were barbequing. He dashed into the house, slamming the door open and running past the entryway without taking off his shoes.

"Annie!" He called. No answer. "Annie?!" His heart was rattling. Did a robber break in? I knew I should have added another lock to the door after I was so easily getting into the house the first time I met Philippa.

"Uncle Henry!" Annie ran down the stairs and threw herself onto him, burying her face in his stomach.

"What happened? Where's Charlie? Where's Philippa?" At Philippa's name, Annie's shoulders started shaking, and he realized with a sinking feeling that Annie was crying. He crouched lower so he could look into her red eyes. "What happened?"

"Annie, you need to calm down," a male voice that constantly grated on Henry's nerves said. Henry turned to see Horace also descend the stairs, Angela following behind.

"Honey, we'll find someone else to watch you and take you to soccer," Angela came over and lightly patted Annie's head, but Annie shrugged away from her mother.

His sister's words slowly sank in. Someone else to watch them, Annie crying at Philippa's name. No. It can't be. "Annie, where is Philippa?"

Annie looked to the ground as new tears sparked in her eyes. That was enough of an answer to make Henry's veins burn with the desire to fix the problem.

"Philippa will not be around here anymore," Horace answered, his snobby voice like nails on a chalk board to Henry's ears.

"We've decided to let her go," Angela continued for her soon to be ex-husband.

Henry froze. "You let her go?" Annie snuffled beside him. "Why would you let her go? I thought you said she was the best babysitter you've ever had?"

"She put her values before our words, setting the kids against us," Horace gestured to Annie, who was keeping Henry between her parents and her.

"Her values? Philippa values family above all else, except God."

"It's true," Angela said, further shocking Henry. "She was setting them against us."

Angela, Angie, Henry's sister was stating the most idiotic thing he had ever heard. Perhaps if he hadn't spent so much time with Philippa and the kids, he would immediately take his sister's word for it, but he knew Philippa. He knew she wanted nothing more than to see this family heal and become whole again. "Annie, please go upstairs." Henry put a hand through his hair as his mind began to analyze the problem and the best solution. The problem was simple; there was a misunderstanding between Philippa and Horace and Angela. The solution was more complicated. He needed to find the misunderstanding, help them to come to a new conclusion, then have them get over their pride and rehire her. Which was not likely, but he had to try. For everyone's sanity.

Once Annie was up the steps, the three of them sat on the couch, Horace and Angela sitting together while Henry sat across from them.

"What happened? And give me details."

"Why do you need details?" Horace asked. "They are not your kids. I've appreciated your help over these past few weeks, but they are not your children."

"I need the details because your kids are going to come to me for answers, and I would like to understand the problem from all points of view before I even try to give them answers. So, please begin."

"Well," Angela began, looking down at her hands that sat gracefully in her lap. Henry wished she'd talk with her hands. She used to when they were younger, but over the years she had stamped out the habit. "Philippa and the children came home from school shopping while Horace and I were having a discussion-"

"A fight, Angie," Henry sighed.

"It was a discussion," Angie insisted.

"Was there yelling involved?" Henry took her silence as a yes. "If there is yelling then that means it's a fight. Don't mix up your words, or you're going to cause problems for the children in the future. Let's be blunt, if you will." This should be Philippa's job. She would be much more eloquent with her words. Much more graceful about all of this. "So, they came in while you were fighting, what happened next?"

"We told the children to go up to their room," Horace answered, rubbing the bridge of his nose where his reading glasses usually sat. "We didn't want them to be caught in the middle of the fight. I then told Philippa she could go home."

"You did not!" Angie shrilled. "You kept going with the fight."

"The fact that she didn't leave had nothing to do with me."

"You didn't give her the chance to get out before you started it up again!"

Their voices were rising, so Henry put his hand in the air to pause them. "The kids can hear everything, so please keep your voices down. So, Philippa was present while you two were having a personal fight," the words sickened Henry. Philippa didn't have a mean bone in her body, and being put in that situation was probably mortifying to her. "So, whose side did she choose, and why did the other take such offense that they fired her?"

"She didn't pick sides. She simply had some opinions about our divorce that didn't sit well with us. She was respectful in how she presented her concerns, but we recognized the ideas put us in a bad light and that she was putting the children against us."

"As proven by how dramatic Annie has been this afternoon," Horace added.

"So," Henry let the words sit on its own for a moment. "You fired her because of her beliefs about divorce?"

"She's setting the kids against us, Henry," Angela sighed, finally making eye contact with him. "The divorce is hard enough as it is, but to have her whispering in their ears makes it even worse."

"Annie has been angry with us since before Philippa came to help, and Charlie has been despondent. Philippa is making things more complicated and worse for them. We had to do what was best for the family." Horrace said, looking only at Angela.

Henry was silent for a moment as he pondered his words. "Charlie has been despondent?" Both Angela and Horace nod. "Since coming here, I have only seen Charlie despondent twice- both times were when you two were fighting. I have spent an enormous amount of time with the kids this summer, along with their babysitter. I have heard nearly everything she has said to them. Not a single word has been against you. She has put all of her time and energy into being a constant for the kids. Call me crazy, but I highly doubt she has ever, or ever would, say anything against you."

Henry got up from his spot and headed for the front door.

"Where are you going?" Angela called.

"I'm going to Philippa's to see if she's okay. Because she loves those kids as if they were part of her family, and you have just cut them off from her."

"I understand you are sympathetic," Horace sighed, weariness weighing on his shoulders, "But I'm not offering her the job again. With the trial in a month, I think a fresh start will be good for everyone."

Henry wanted to strangle Horace. Henry had never been a big fan of the man. But in this moment, his rage stopped almost as instantly as it had begun. Horace looked tired. Bags under his eyes, a shock of premature gray hair making its way through the sides of his head, and his whole body slouched. It was true that Horace could be a pain, but Henry also knew that Angela could be one too. Horace had never lifted a hand against her, never been unfaithful, and even now he was thinking about the kids. Henry swallowed the annoyance that threatened to bubble out of him and instead nodded his head. "If that is what you wish."

Henry left the house and entered his truck, letting the dark roads lit only by streetlights guide him to his destination.

"Hello?" Philippa's small voice called through the door.

Oh, this is definitely not good. She always opens the door. It's part of her too trusting manner. "Philippa, it's me, Henry." The door opened a crack, allowing him to see just the corner of her red face. "Oh, Philippa."

A tear slid down her cheek, but she brushed it away quickly. She silently opened the door all the way, moving to let him in. He had never seen the inside of her apartment, just small flashes whenever she came out. But the inside matched her personality. The white carpeted entryway stretched over to what Henry assumed was the living room. The living room was small, with only a couch and floral coffee table. There wasn't even a TV. The large window that took up the side of her living room let streams of moonlight in, filtered through sheer curtains with sunflowers embroidered upon them. The kitchen, which was to the left of the entryway, was simple and small. White cabinets, a fridge, and a stove with a small amount of counter space would have looked completely plain and ordinary if Philippa hadn't strung fishing wire through flowers to hang from the cabinet to the counter as a sort of barrier.

He kicked his shoes off and placed them neatly beside the door next to her tennis shoes. Philippa took a breath and crossed her arms. Now that the door wasn't in the way, he took in her light purple sweatpants and her oversized white sweatshirt. Her long silky black hair that was so dark it usually reflected a hint of blue, was pulled into a large mop of a bun that was only held together by the red pen that she carried with her everywhere.

"This is the living room," she gestured to the couch. "That's the kitchen. If you get hungry, you can just grab something. The bathroom is the door to the right," she pointed to the small hall directly opposite him. "These are the only rooms you're allowed in. If you go into my bedroom, I will kick you out."

It was the first time Henry had ever heard her be so strict, but he appreciated that she had boundaries. "Understood," he nodded.

Philippa's shoulders lowered in relief, and she turned to the kitchen. "Have a seat, I'll brew some tea. Is there a flavor you prefer?"

Henry wasn't a very big fan of tea, but he knew that she would feel better if she had a cup of tea in her hands, and she wouldn't drink if he wouldn't. "Do you have peppermint?"

"Yes, I'll get started on that right away."

Instead of going to the couch to sit, he went to the other side of the counter so he could watch her make tea through the flowers that dangled between them. She raised an eyebrow at him but didn't say anything. Her lack of words wasn't new to him. She likes to think more than speak. But still…she usually is more talkative than this. There was something bright about Philippa. She was almost always smiling, her personality that was as sweet as her sweet tea was always shining, and her kindness was just an envelope of warmth. But her smile was gone, as was the bright light that always shined in her eyes. Her movements were smooth and efficient as she got her water started and pulled tea from her ironing board. Any other day, he would ask why she hung her tea on the ironing board, but not today.

"You have a beautiful apartment." It was small talk, and he normally didn't like small talk, but the compliment was true, and he was grasping at straws to get some sign of life out of her.

"Thank you. I've always loved decorating. I just added the flower curtain," a spoon in her hand, she tapped the flowers hanging from the fishing wire.

"It suits you."

"Thank you," she murmured, going back into her silence.

Within a few moments they both had tea in their hands and were sitting on her couch, a proper distance between them. He longed to close that distance and grab her hand, but that would be intruding, something he definitely didn't want to be. So, he took a sip of the burning peppermint tea and waited for her to speak.

It was several moments before she finally whispered, "I suppose you heard about my employment, or lack thereof."

"Yes. I'm so sorry, Philippa. I know you love Annie and Charlie."

"It's okay. I've been thinking about it a lot, and I suppose that it is for the best. No, I know it's for the best. God's plan is far better than mine." She sipped at her tea; her voice growing stronger as she talked. "Things were going to change soon, anyway. School will begin soon, and it is far better for them to have someone who can focus on them and their needs instead of being in a rush, grading papers."

Henry sat on the thought. "Well, you're right. God's plan is best. I'm thankful that you shared your opinion with my sister and brother-in-law. I hope that they will remember your words, and maybe it will change their point of view."

Philippa nodded but pressed her lips together. "It was awful, Henry. They were so loud; Charlie and Annie had become so pale. I just wanted them to be more mindful of what they were doing, but now I fear that I've done more damage than anything else."

"You can't do more damage to them. They are already ready for a divorce, nothing you could have said could have split them up more."

Philippa sighed and looked out the window. "You'll keep me updated on them, I hope? Unless you want to stop dating, as it would likely make things more awkward for you?" She looked him in the eye, completely steady, but he didn't miss the tremble in her voice.

He lightly placed his hand on hers. She turned her wrist, so their palms touched while her fingers wrapped around his. Her hand was warm from holding her tea for so long, but he basked in that warmth. "How could I stop something so beautiful from growing?

This thing between us is worth caring for. It's like a flower. Sure, it takes some work, but all that work is worth it when it turns into something that shines with beauty. This thing between us may be hard to nurture but it's worth it."

Philippa nodded, her glassy eyes meeting his, and he found in that moment that he would do anything to keep her by his side. To protect her from the world and all the tears that came with it. He would fight every battle to be with her and to keep her safe. He hadn't realized they were so close, but now he felt like there was a magnet that was pulling him closer. No, no, no. I need to have control and keep her pure until I have a ring on her finger.

"So why don't you have a TV?" he stuttered.

Philippa pulled back and laughed. "Why is that always what people want to know?"

He chuckled. "I just haven't met anyone who didn't have a TV front and center in their house."

"Ah, well I originally couldn't afford one, then I found I didn't need it. I have a computer if I need some simple entertainment, and Charice gave me a key and permanent permission to use her TV whenever I want to. Usually, the two of us binge watch movies every other Wednesday after prayer, and then I just spend the night."

"That sounds fun."

"Much better than watching a movie on my own in my little living room."

Dreams of them watching movies on a big screen in a living room they called their own filled him, making his head spin with what if's. I need to get out of here. It's not good for me to be this close to her all on our own. A few more minutes and I don't know how well my control will be. This tea and long day are making my senses too dull.

"I should be going, if you are certain you're alright?"

Philippa nodded. "Charice is supposed to come over after her shift, so she should be here in twenty minutes."

"That's good. I'll call you tomorrow. Unfortunately, I don't have time to get lunch with you tomorrow, but how about dinner?"

"I can't. I'm helping with the worship team's practice tomorrow. But I'll see you at church on Sunday."

A little disheartened to have to wait until Sunday, he nodded. "Until Sunday."

He went through the door and stood in the night air as he listened to Philippa's steps through the door. God, please give her strength this night. I know this is affecting her more than she's saying it is.

Two weeks later.

"Angela, this can't be good for the children."

Henry stopped before turning the corner at the sound of Horace's voice.

"What do you mean? We're this close to being done."

"But I don't think it's right. The kids are depressed all the time, and what we're about to put them through with split custody..." Horace sighed.

Angela sighed. "I know. They're quieter than they have been. Did you know they still eat together in the dining room?"

"Six o'clock. Every night."

"What do you suggest we do?"

"I don't know. I just keep thinking over Ms. Carol's words. They keep echoing in my head, and I've been wondering if there's some truth to them."

"But you, you're the one who suggested the divorce!" Angela whisper-shouted.

"And you shut Ms. Carol down and said our marriage wasn't salvageable. But both of those things happened while we were angry. Maybe we should look into one of the options we've been avoiding."

"Pastor Tom?"

Henry backed away slowly, his feet moving without his permission. This needs to be their decision. I shouldn't be eavesdropping. But thank You God for giving me this small snippet of hope. Henry turned to the entryway; his feet lighter than they had been in months. I need to hurry. I can't be late to take Philippa to her first mini golf game.

CHAPTER TWENTY-EIGHT

2⁶ "Philippa, it's been two weeks. What do you need me to do to help get rid of your sadness?" Charice asked, holding her coffee cup close.

The morning was cloudy, the sun's beams diluting into gray. Philippa was walking with Charice for Charice's morning stroll before going to work. With Philippa's unemployment, she suddenly found she had too many free hours, so she now followed her friends around a bit. The morning walk was a little silly since it was just from Charice's house to the coffee shop three blocks away.

"That's sweet, but I don't think there is anything you could do."

Charice sighed. "I thought you'd say that."

"School is starting next week. Once I get back into my routine with teaching, everything will get easier." It was all that was keeping Philippa going at this point. *I knew that I couldn't watch them forever. I just wish that there was some way to help them.* The sting of being let go had faded to nothing but a dull ache. What took over her thoughts at all hours of the day was Annie and Charlie's pain. *They're not alone. Henry told me he was watching them for now. He will help them. They aren't going to go through this alone.*

"That's true. Though I will miss our morning walks."

Philippa laughed. "You're just going to miss having a good excuse to buy coffee."

"It certainly doesn't hurt. Are you ready to get back to teaching?"

"Almost. I just have to finish decorating my classroom, which I was planning to do tonight. You can come too, if you want."

"Why not?" Charice bumped Philippa's shoulder as she swung her free hand at her side.

"Charice," Philippa dragged the name out as she wondered how to phrase her question. "Do you think we'll still be friends in five years?"

"Yep," Charice said, not even hesitating. "The only reason we wouldn't be is if you decided to kidnap and murder people, and even then, I'm sure you'd have your reasons. Who knows, maybe I'd be helping you hide the bodies. Why do you ask?"

"I don't know. I guess I'm just having a hard time leaving my comfort zone."

"In what way?"

"Missions."

"Ah," Charice nodded, knowingly.

"I know that I want to go. I know that this is where God is calling me. But it's just so hard to venture into the unknown. I don't want to leave this life that I've built here. Things are so great here, even after the Johnsons let me go."

They walked in silence as Charice thought through Philippa's words. "Whatever you choose, it's going to be hard."

Philippa stopped walking. *No one has said that one yet.* Charice stopped beside her but kept talking. "Life here isn't always going to be so simple or easy. There are going to be hard spots. Missions aren't going to be easy. You can't go just because you think you should. You have to be strong. You're not living for yourself out there. Every day a new trial will rise, and you are going to see suffering in a deeper sense than you know. But if you are dedicated and strong enough, pray for God to give you the strength to leap. If you don't think you can do it, then remain here and build a different kind of ministry than you were originally thinking of. Both options are going to be hard. It's not an easy decision, but you must decide sooner rather than later."

She's right. I can't keep dragging my feet about this. I need to choose my hard.

"Oh, but we better hurry back to my house," Charice said, looking at her smart watch. "I have to get going to work in half an hour, and if I don't grab another cup of coffee then we are going to be in big trouble."

"The one in your hand isn't enough?" Philippa smiled as she began walking again.

"Of course not, I have presentations today. If all goes well, then I will only be there for one more week before moving to a different company. I have to make sure everything goes perfectly, and for that to happen, I have to have enough caffeine in me to load a tank." Charice lifted her hand to massage her temple. "Just thinking of them is giving me a headache. Scratch the coffee. I'm making a cortado."

"Isn't a cortado a kind of coffee?"

"Girl, I think that is the single most offensive thing I've ever heard."

Philippa giggled and bumped Charice's shoulder. "Thanks."

"Anytime."

"Oh, goodness. Why is this so hard?" Philippa grumbled as she leaned her head on Henry's shoulder.

"I'm pretty sure all that you have to do is hit the send button. I'm not sure how hard that is," he chuckled.

The two were sitting in a booth at the local coffee shop and looking at Philippa's laptop. The setting sun was sending rays of burning orange through the windows and between the leaves of all the plants that were artfully shoved into the window. The café was mostly empty, but there were enough people to leave a hum of chatter.

It's just a button, and I've already made my decision. Philippa leaned forward and pushed the button, the click of the mouse like thunder as she watched the load screen take her to the *your response has been successfully submitted* screen.

"I did it!" Philippa smiled as she leaned back into her seat.

"Congratulations, Miss Missionary," Henry smiled down at her.

"Are you sure you're fine with me leaving for a different country for a whole year? How are we going to do long distance?" *I can't believe I find a really great guy and then choose to leave him behind for a year. But oddly, leaving isn't so scary anymore.* A gentle peace filled her as some of her favorite Bible verses came to mind.

"Don't worry about it. I have a few ideas, but tonight we're going to celebrate this opportunity you've been given."

"I can't believe I finally made my decision!" Philippa giggled.

"We should go bowling to celebrate."

"You just want to go bowling because you know I can't beat you. How about we go mini golfing instead."

"Now that's just playing unfair. How was I to know you had a secret superpower in golf?"

"You just shouldn't have underestimated me," Philippa laughed as she put her laptop into her bag. "Oh, but Henry." She waited for him to look at her. "I've been thinking about it, and I would appreciate it if you told me how the kids are doing, but don't tell me anything about the divorce. I know it's going to happen, but I want to stay out of it like they asked me to."

Henry nodded slowly. "If that's what you want."

"It is." She fixed her glasses. "Thank you for being there for them. I know they're your family, but not everyone would do that. Weren't you expected to return home by now?"

"I was supposed to go back last week," he conceded. "But I told them that I needed to be here for my family. I didn't tell them I had more than one reason for staying here."

Philippa blushed. "Ah, yes, well, um." *Why does he make my thoughts a puddle?!* "I mean, they were okay with it?"

"Kind of. They just switched some of my projects with another guy, and so I'll be working here for a little longer. I probably have until October when the snow starts to fall. I'll either have to find a different job or go back. I'm going to see how things are here before I make any rash decisions."

"Makes sense." Philippa smiled as she hopped out of the booth. "Let's go to the mini golf course!"

Henry groaned as he joined her on the stroll to the door, opening it before she could get to it. "If we have to."

"We do."

CHAPTER TWENTY-NINE

The first month after getting fired had been sad, but that sadness quickly changed to excitement over the new school year. Her new class was extremely chaotic, but Philippa reveled in getting back to a routine. The month after that was a quiet time full of anxiety. The Johnsons' case was likely over by now, but she had no answers as to how it had turned out. Charlie had once tried to sneak over to her class after school one day, but Mr. Johnson was quick to pick him up and head back home. She longed to feel Charlie's hugs again. She missed Annie desperately. She missed being part of their lives. It had been four months since Philippa had been fired from the Johnson's home. In those four months, Philippa's life settled back into the old routine of the school year.

It was a Thursday when she ran into Mrs. White's classroom after school with a paper raised high above her head. "They've just sent me where I'll be stationed and what I will be teaching!"

"Oh, good. I was afraid of growing impatient," Mrs. White said, maneuvering around the small desks to stand beside Philippa. She took the paper and looked it over. "This is very exciting."

"It's all becoming very real," Philippa pulled her hair behind her ear. It felt like just yesterday that she was showing Mrs. White her acceptance into the program on the last day of school. But that had been months ago, and so much had changed since then.

"I'm sure it is. But I'm so proud of you. We all are. I'll miss you so much," Mrs. White's eyes filled with tears.

Philippa wrapped her arms around the old woman and squeezed her in a hug. "Thank you, Mrs. White. You've taught me so much about being a teacher, a part of the community, and being a friend. I'm going to miss you. However, we still have a few months together, and then I'll only be gone for a year."

Mrs. White pulled back and took Philippa's hands in her own, patting them lightly, her weathered soft fingers giving warmth to Philippa. "I know. We must be joyful while we still have you. Perhaps you could come over tomorrow night? Calvin can make some of his world-famous burgers."

Philippa opened her mouth to speak when a knock sounded at Mrs. White's classroom door. Both women turned to find Mrs. Johnson at the door.

"Angela?" Mrs. White raised an eyebrow but went in to hug her.

"Hello, Gwen," Mrs. Johnson smiled at Mrs. White.

"Why have you graced us with your presence today? Don't you have to get your kids home?"

"Actually, I am here to talk with Ms. Carol."

Philippa blinked in surprise. "Me?"

"Yes. Would you walk over a couple of halls with me to pick up Charlie? I'd like to have a talk with you."

Oh dear. What did I do? No. She couldn't have anything bad to talk about if we're just strolling through the school. Unease thundered through her, but Philippa put on her teacher's smile and nodded. "Of course. Lead the way."

Philippa and Mrs. Johnson had only made it past the classroom door when Mrs. Johnson spoke. "Ms. Carol, I must apologize for everything that happened all those months ago."

Philippa paused, her natural responses failing her as her eyebrows rose to the ceiling. *That is not at all what I thought she was going to say.* "I beg your pardon?"

Mrs. Johnson kept walking, making Philippa skip a step back into motion. "Horrace and I had tried therapy, but it didn't work. We had lived with the fighting for over a year before we finally began the paperwork for divorce. I love Horrace, but that love had been buried underneath a lot of hurt and frustration. One of Pastor Tom's sermons had said we were to forgive our enemies, and I knew I couldn't forgive Horrace. He didn't deserve any grace." Mrs. Johnson stopped fully and turned to look Philippa in the eye, her forest green eyes a mirror of her daughter's. "But then you said that we had to have grace for each other. I will admit, those words had me steaming mad. I had gone to Gwen's house the next day and complained to her and told her what you said."

"I had assumed," Mrs. Johnson began walking again, "that she would agree with me and help me to vent everything out. A small part of me hoped she would reprimand you. But instead, she asked me if I deserved grace. We talked for hours about how Jesus Christ bled for me. Sin, something I hadn't ever truly cared about, was separating me from God. I was undeserving of grace, and yet the God of all creation sent his beloved Son to die for me." Mrs. Johnson sniffled, and Philippa tentatively put her hand on her elbow to give some sense of comfort. "I have heard a million times that the Son of God died for the unworthy, but I never truly understood or saw it in that light. I could never send my sweet Charlie or my beautiful Annie out to die. Even for a worthy person! But God sent His Son for me."

"Gwen and I worked through everything for a couple of weeks and prayed for my marriage to be saved. Oh, Ms. Carol, I had never been so desperate on my knees. Then one day, Horrace told me he had been thinking about what you said."

Philippa paused, afraid to breathe. "And?" she prompted.

"We are still together Ms. Carol."

Philippa smiled wide. *Thank You, Lord.* In her joy she hugged Mrs. Johnson, squeezing her in tight. "Oh, that is wonderful news!"

"Ms. Carol!" Charlie's little voice squealed as he ran from his class, which was just a door down, and hugged her. Philippa shifted her hug from Mrs. Johnson to Charlie, his small figure a little bigger than before but familiar in her embrace.

"Charlie!" A tear slid down her cheek as she clung to him.

"Pip!" Philippa turned her head to see Annie running over from the entry doors, a smile lighting her eyes.

"Annie?! What are you doing here?" Though she was questioning, Philippa still scooped her into a hug.

"Mom picked me up before Charlie and told me to wait at the door. Did you hear? Momma and Dad didn't get separated! We still live in the same house, and we still play games after dinner!"

Mrs. Johnson cleared her throat. "Yes. I moved my schedule to working two days a week. It helps me to see my patients that truly need me while also being with my family."

"And Dad always comes home early to make dinner with Momma!" Charlie added.

"That is fantastic news." Philippa looked Annie in the eyes. "I am so happy for you," She turned her gaze to Charlie and Mrs. Johnson. "All of you."

"Thank you," Mrs. Johnson smiled as she hoisted Charlie onto her hip. "For caring for my kids and for Horrace and me. I hope you can join us this weekend to play a few board games."

Thank You, God, for Your beautiful plan in these lives that I was blessed to witness. Your mercies are truly new every morning. "Always."

Chapter Thirty

The night was cold, and the air was caught in flurries of snow. Philippa smiled over at Henry as he approached her with the mini golf clubs and balls. The mini golf course was outdoors, and though there had been two snowstorms just in time for Christmas, the courses were shoveled clean with only a freckle of snow on them.

"I cannot believe you wanted to do this?" Philippa pushed up her glasses as she led the way to the first round. It was a simple straight line to the hole, but it had a pretty, little castle and carriage in the corner of it.

"Yes, well, if you are going to be leaving soon, then I have to try and beat you at least once in this silly game." He pulled his scarf up over his nose, making his words a little muffled.

"I can understand that part, but why did you choose to go mini golfing when it's fifteen degrees out?" Philippa hit her ball perfectly into the hole, the sinking sound a beautiful melody.

Henry hit his ball with too much force, the ball bouncing across the hole, hitting the back curb, ricocheting back to the hole where it spun down into an odd victory. "I was hoping the cold would mess with your swing, but it seems to have left you alone and instead messed with me."

Philippa giggled as she went to the next hole. "You should have known better." She hit the ball into the hole. The same with the next one. And the one after that. But as they got farther through the course, the more everything looked different. The hole that had an alligator on it, now had a frying pan in the plastic animal's mouth.

"That's odd," Philippa pointed to it, but Henry just smiled and shrugged.

"It must be their fun way of keeping things new."

"I suppose."

The next hole with the pirate ship had a pot of steaming chili in it. Philippa, as she grabbed her ball from the hole, studied the pot. "Does this look like Charice's pot?" The steam lifted to her nose, making her cough at the heavily spiced scent. "It smells like her chili."

Philippa furrowed her eyebrows at Henry, but he just continued to smile. "Maybe she forgot it here. Come on, let's go to the next hole. I want to beat you before they close."

At the sound of competition, Philippa sprung back into action as she made her way to the next hole. The next wasn't too unusual. Instead of the race car that was typically above the hole, it was a dark wooden gazebo. *I've seen this gazebo before. But where?* Philippa pushed the question aside. *I must keep my eyes on the prize. I'm not sure when this place closes, but it is pretty late, and it will drive me crazy if we've made it this far and don't finish.* Philippa sunk the hole, and Henry took three tries to do the same. *That's odd. He usually gets that in one go. Maybe the cold is getting to him.*

"Henry, if you're cold, we can go home and try this again some other, warmer, time." Leaving early didn't feel right, but Henry catching a cold because of her competitiveness would have made her feel a million times worse.

Henry's eyes widened and he jumped. "Oh, no. No, I am completely fine, but thank you for asking. Besides, I'm feeling good about this next one."

Philippa raised an eyebrow at him but followed. The next hole was odd as it had a long stringy pizza on top of a whale's head, but Philippa just smiled at it. This wasn't even the oddest one.

"Doesn't that pizza look like the one we got from Mouse and Cheese?" Henry casually said as he hit his ball with his blue club.

The hole after that had red, white, and blue flowers lining the curbs. The next hole had little knickknacks that Philippa KNEW she had seen before. It itched her brain as she waited for Henry to finish his turn before it finally clicked. *Oh! A couple of vendors at the farmers' market sell these. How nice that the golf course is using them for decoration!*

However, it was the final hole that made Philippa completely freeze. The little village of plastic houses that were used to make the hole more challenging now had a tiny bush maze that led to a picnic.

"How completely odd." Philippa looked down at the plastic bushes as she retrieved her ball from the hole.

Henry ignored her and pointed to what was almost always a dark alleyway that she assumed led to the employee's lounge or something, but tonight was lit with strings of golden Christmas lights. "This must be a bonus round. Come on."

Philippa only hesitated for a moment before following. "Are you sure it's okay if we go over here? I thought it was employees only—" The words died on her tongue as she stared at the lights that swirled around and an arrow of light pointed down the path.

Something about the whole night had been off. Henry calling her last minute to ask if she would go with him to mini golf. The course having weird and unrelated decorations like a gazebo and a frying pan. *Wait a minute! I know that gazebo! It looks exactly like the one behind the library. I can't believe I didn't recognize it immediately! Henry and I go there almost daily… Oh goodness. Henry! The frying pan is like when we first met. The pizza was from Charlie's birthday. The red, white, and blue flowers are like the ones that had originally been in that vase at the store. The one that Henry had given me filled with his own flowers. And the farmers' market was our first date! And the picnic! Oh, how could I have not recognized the picnic.* Thoughts fluttered through Philippa as she felt like electricity was running through her veins. Her steps were getting heavier as everything was beginning to make sense.

Henry's gloved hand enveloped hers, and he pulled her along the next few steps as he smiled down at her. She opened her mouth to ask him what was going on but froze when they turned the corner.

People – from church, from her work, and from her community services –fanned around the sides and back of the alley, large colorful glow sticks in their hands. Philippa's eyes bulged at the sight of Teressa and Charice holding hands and beaming at her. The shock of everyone being there was nothing compared to the lightning that danced with the butterflies in her stomach. She turned to Henry, who was no longer standing next to her, but instead was kneeling.

"Philippa Carol, you inspire me daily. You make me laugh, bring me to prayer in everything, and have made me a better man. I want to be with you for every sunrise, and I want to chase every sunset with you by my side. I want to fight every battle it takes to love you. We will fight and cry because of each other, but you are worth every tear, every hurt, and every prayer. Will you do me the highest honor and marry me?"

Tears flooded Philippa's eyes as she melted down to hug him, breathing in his scent as she placed her head on his shoulder. "Yes. In every language, tongue, and syllable. Yes!"

She laughed as he picked her up off her feet and spun her around. The air was full of cheering and tears. He placed her lightly down in front of him and pulled out a red velvet box, flipping it open to reveal a gold ring with pink gemstones gathered to resemble a flower. Charice and Teressa were jumping and squealing, while Mrs. White and Calvin smiled at her, and the Johnson family laughed and cried. Henry swooped her up in his arms, princess style, and gave a holler of victory. Philippa laughed but kept her eyes glued on him. His face mirrored her own smile.

In that moment Philippa knew that she was filled to the brim with joy and love.

CHAPTER THIRTY-ONE

The wedding date was set for May. May had seemed so far away at the time, but after tons of florists, venue tours, and caterers, the day was suddenly here. May 24th had bloomed into the present, and Philippa was a ball of nerves as she waited outside the doors of the sanctuary. At any moment the pianist would start playing music, and her bridal party would begin their procession in. In a few moments, she would be Mrs. Philippa Sulivan.

"Take some deep breaths," Charice suggested.

Charice, her maid of honor, looked lovely in her light green dress that flowed like water to the ground. Teressa came over in her matching dress and adjusted Philippa's long floral veil.

"Charice is right, Pip. Take some breaths and just enjoy. You look stunning."

Philippa smiled at her sister, the small girl who used to crawl in the mud, now a vision of a young woman. Philippa looked at her reflection and lightly touched the fabric of her gown. The cream dress hugged her torso with floral embroidery, the long flowing skirt with its many petticoats circled around her, and the flower embroidery strong at the bottom of her skirts but fading into the rest of the smooth fabric as it got higher up the skirt. It was everything, and so much more than, she had ever dreamed.

School had ended on Wednesday and Philippa felt bittersweet about it being her last traditional class for a year. In two weeks, she and Henry would be leaving for China. It hadn't taken Henry long to find out that the community she would be working in was struggling with agriculture, and he wanted to help. He had campaigned with several churches and was now being sent out officially with her as a missionary. *I can't believe the mountains of grace God has rained down upon me.*

Piano music softly filled the room, ripping Philippa from her thoughts of the future. She took a deep breath and watched as her procession took one step slowly at a time. Annie, in her more modest version of the green dress, began the bridesmaid march, her face glowing with pride.

Dear Heavenly Father, I thank You for Your goodness. Your providence and love are a sight to behold. May You guide Henry and me through this next adventure in life. Amen.

Her prayer finished, she allowed her feet to follow the steps of the march. Familiar and unfamiliar faces smiled at her, but that did nothing to help her nerves. Even in her heels, she wasn't tall enough to look over the crowd to find the pair of eyes she wanted to see most. All those eyes staring at her, and the momentous change she was about to marry into, it was all crashing down on her. *No. I can't think like this. I need to focus on something else.* Philippa stared at

Charice's green gown, letting the way it shone in the candlelight distract her. She only looked up for a moment but still couldn't see Henry over all the heads that were around her. *Wait. There!* Henry, with his glowing eyes, found her, and everything around her slowly melted away. As she stood on the stage with Henry and Pastor Tom, everything clicked into place.

"We gather here to celebrate the union of Philippa Carol and Henry Sulivan. Could the bride's parents rise." Philippa's mother and father rose in the front seats, as did a majority of her side of the church. What's going on? "Do you give your daughter to this fine man, to cherish and to hold until death they do part?"

"We do!" Almost the whole church sang. Tears sprung in Philippa's eyes, and she was suddenly thankful for the waterproof mascara. The rest of the ceremony passed as it had in rehearsal, at least that's what Philippa assumed. She couldn't seem to see or think straight as she looked into Henry's eyes and felt his warm hand take hers and place a gold ring above her engagement ring. Rather than a regular second ring, her wedding band curved around the diamonds of her engagement ring and had green gems cut to look like the leaves of her diamond flower. She placed his ring on his finger, placing her public claim on him.

"With the power vested in me," Pastor Tom smiled, "I now pronounce you man and wife. You may now kiss the bride."

Henry put his hand on her waist, electricity flowing from where he was touching her, and his other hand came up and cupped her cheek. He leaned in and kissed her. The kiss was soft but brought sunlight to their lips as his warmth grew into her. Everything was muted, and all she knew was that Henry was who she was destined to be with.

They pulled apart and faced the crowd that was loud with cheers and tears.

Henry leaned down and kissed her cheek, keeping his lips there as he whispered, "Off we go to our next adventure."

She pulled to the side just enough to smile at him. "To wherever God leads us."

Philippa had barely finished her sentence when Henry gave her another knee-knocking kiss.

Chapter Thirty-Two

A house of white stood in a field of flowers. The wooden two-story house stood pristine with its pastel shutters and wraparound porch. Beside the light green door was a large two-seater porch swing, swinging in the breeze. A large black Labrador trotted around the house, heading toward the back yard. It followed the small rock path that led to a waist high wooden fence with a swinging door that the dog pushed right through. The fence held a garden that bloomed with flowers of all scents and colors. In the middle of this garden was Philippa.

Philippa wore a plain cotton blue dress with a sun hat adorned by a flower. The blue cotton dress flowed down her but couldn't hide the large bump that had become Philippa's stomach. She leaned down to cut a purple flower and placed it neatly in her basket as the black lab ran into her legs.

"Woah, calm down Lucy," Philippa giggled at the dog and petted her head, much to Lucy's delight.

"Why, hello there," A male voice sang over to her.

"Henry!" She ran over and threw herself into Henry's arms.

"Picking flowers I see," he said into the top of her hair.

"They're for my ladies' Bible study later. They always love it when they get to see our flowers."

"I thought today's was at Charice's."

"No, that's next week."

"Ah, that explains it," He leaned down and gave her a kiss that still made her sigh dreamily like a schoolgirl. "Where is our little tornado?"

Hearing the nickname, a small girl, aged three, came spinning out of the flowers, launching herself into her father's outstretched arms. "Daddy!"

"Tornado!"

"She was helping me pick flowers," Philippa said, lifting her basket to show the flowers they had selected. Henry leaned to look at their selections when Philippa jumped a little. "Oh! The baby kicked!"

"Well, if he's anything like our little Tarinthali, then that's only the first of many kicks."

"The baby could be a girl!"

Henry leaned down to listen to her tummy. "Nope, he says he's a boy."

A small splat of dirt hit Henry's cheek. "Uh, oh," Philippa said as Henry picked up a large wad of mud.

"You're going to regret that!"

"Only if you catch me!"

Philippa ran in a fit of giggles, Tarinthali on her heels.

The sunset colored the sky with reds and oranges as Philippa ran from the loves of her life, laughing and praising God for all that He had given her.

The End